# Crush

## Svetlana Chmakova

# Crush

## SVETLANA CHMAKOVA

Coloring assistants: Melissa McCommon, BonHyung Jeong
Inking assistants: NaRae Lee, BonHyung Jeong
Lettering: JuYoun Lee

JY
1290 Avenue of the Americas
New York, NY 10104

Visit us at jyforkids.com
facebook.com/jyforkids
twitter.com/jyforkids
jyforkids.tumblr.com
instagram.com/jyforkids

First JY Edition: October 2018

JY is an imprint of Yen Press, LLC.
The JY name and logo are trademarks of Yen Press, LLC.

The publisher is not responsible for websites (or their content) that are not owned by the publisher.

Library of Congress Control Number: 2018948318

Hardcover ISBN: 978-0-316-36323-5
Paperback ISBN: 978-0-316-36324-2

10 9 8 7 6 5 4 3 2 1

LSC-C

Printed in the United States of America

# Table of Contents

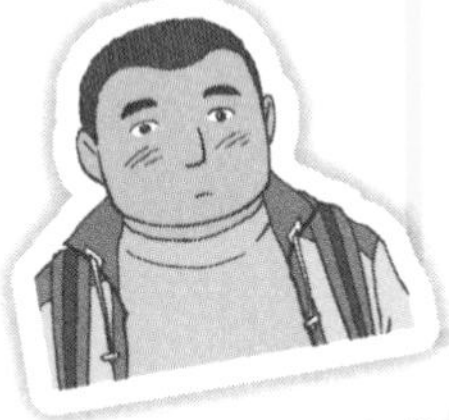
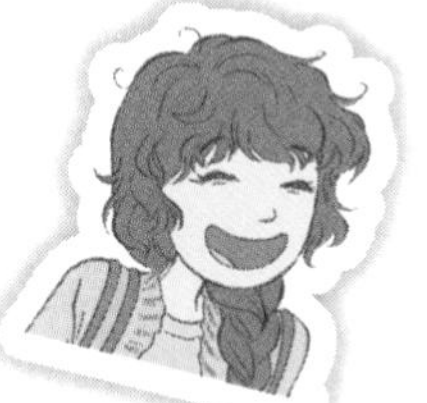



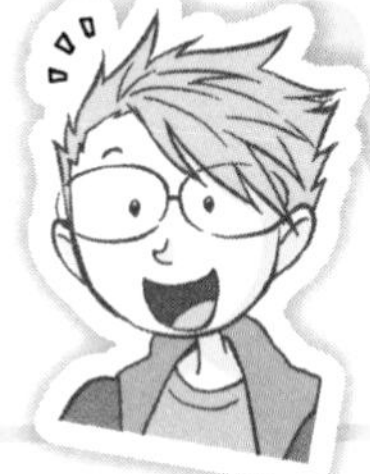
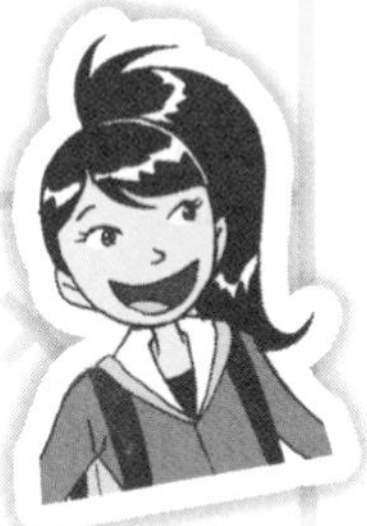
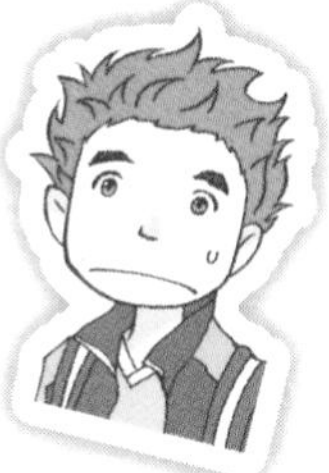
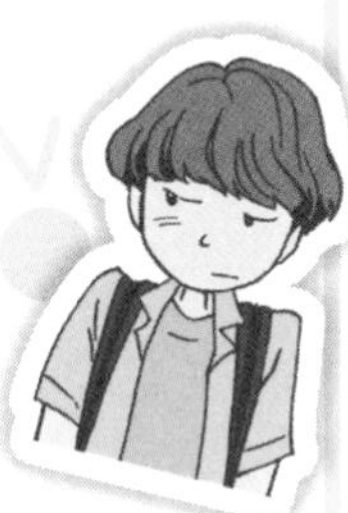

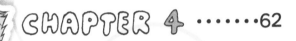

# CHAPTER 1

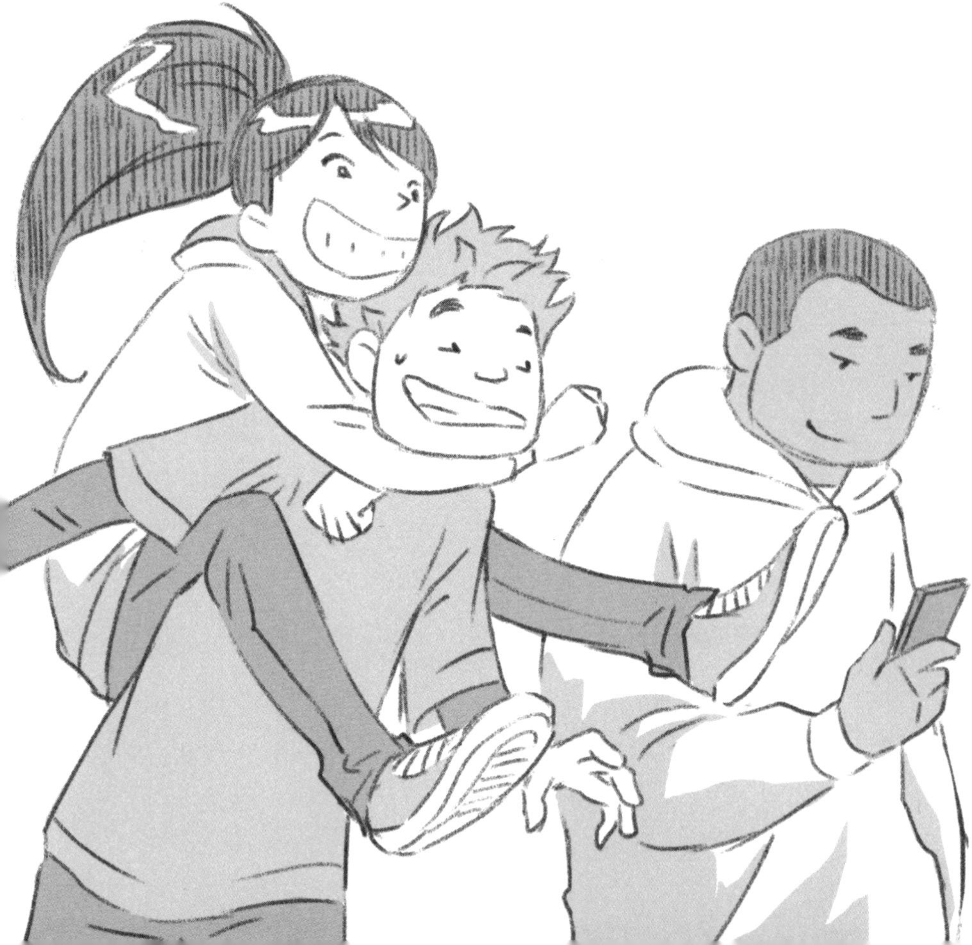

JORGE RUIZ, HERE.

ON THE BUS TO BERRYBROOK MIDDLE SCHOOL, LIKE EVERY MORNING.

(EXCEPT WEEKENDS. THEY HAVEN'T TAKEN THAT FROM US YET, HEH.)

YAMMER

CHATTER

HA HA HA

HA HA

HEY!

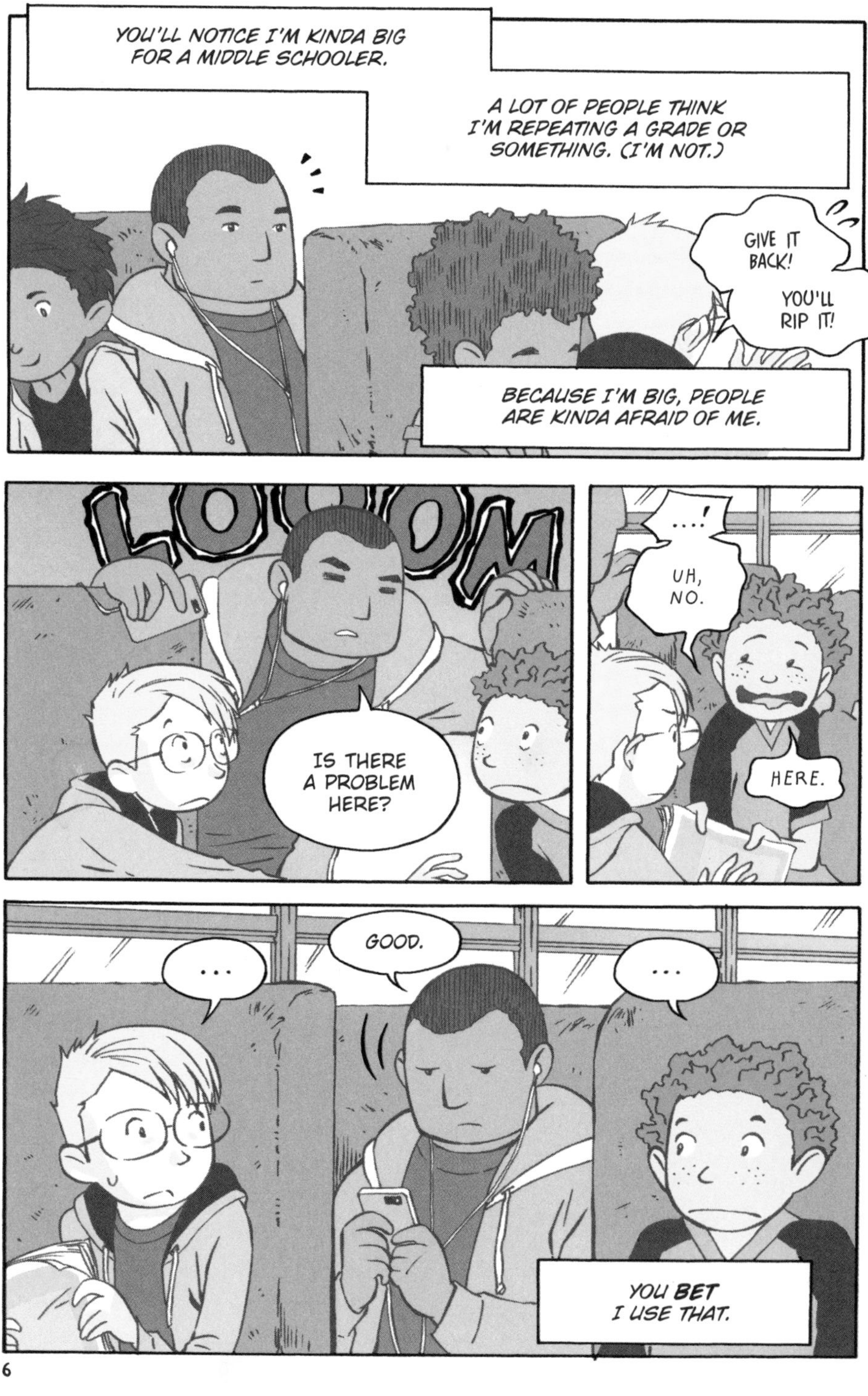
YOU'LL NOTICE I'M KINDA BIG FOR A MIDDLE SCHOOLER.
A LOT OF PEOPLE THINK I'M REPEATING A GRADE OR SOMETHING. (I'M NOT.)
GIVE IT BACK!
YOU'LL RIP IT!
BECAUSE I'M BIG, PEOPLE ARE KINDA AFRAID OF ME.
LOOOM
IS THERE A PROBLEM HERE?
....!
UH, NO.
HERE.
...
GOOD.
...
YOU BET I USE THAT.

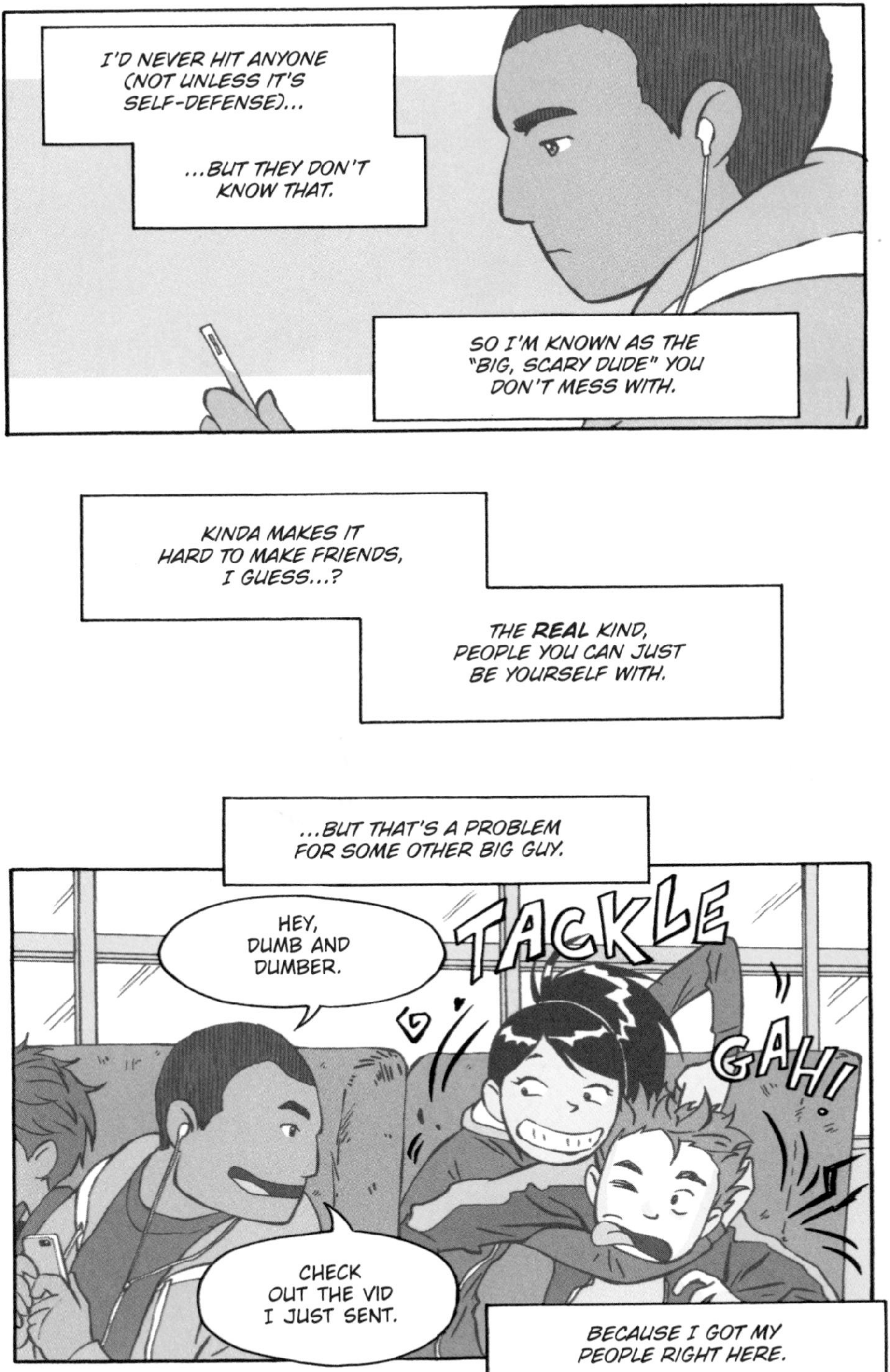
I'D NEVER HIT ANYONE (NOT UNLESS IT'S SELF-DEFENSE)...
...BUT THEY DON'T KNOW THAT.
SO I'M KNOWN AS THE "BIG, SCARY DUDE" YOU DON'T MESS WITH.
KINDA MAKES IT HARD TO MAKE FRIENDS, I GUESS...?
THE **REAL** KIND, PEOPLE YOU CAN JUST BE YOURSELF WITH.
...BUT THAT'S A PROBLEM FOR SOME OTHER BIG GUY.
HEY, DUMB AND DUMBER.
TACKLE
GAH!
CHECK OUT THE VID I JUST SENT.
BECAUSE I GOT MY PEOPLE RIGHT HERE.

THESE TWO CLOWNS—

OMG HAHAHA!!

PFFRT RIP

AHAHA HA THAT'S GOLD!

OLIVIA AND GARRETT, MY BEST FRIENDS SINCE WE ALL THOUGHT THE TOOTH FAIRY WAS REAL.

DID HE JUST FART SO HARD HE SPLIT HIS PANTS?!

LIV AND I HAVE BEEN AT BERRYBROOK SINCE FOREVER, BUT GARRETT ONLY JUST TRANSFERRED TO OUR SCHOOL...

...SO LIV'S BEEN ALL OVER HIM, MAKING SURE HE "FITS RIGHT IN."

BLAH BLAH BLAH

ugh, yes, mooom.

WHICH WORKS FOR ME (BECAUSE PEOPLE FINALLY STOPPED THINKING LIV AND I ARE DATING).

IT WAS SO DUMB.

SHE'S LIKE A SISTER...

...BUT PEOPLE STILL ASSUMED.

AND THIS YEAR ESPECIALLY, THE WHOLE SCHOOL'S OBSESSED— WHO'S DATING WHO, WHO'S ASKING WHO OUT...

IT'S ANNOYING.

WHO'S GOT TIME FOR THAT CRAP?

OH! HI, JORGE!

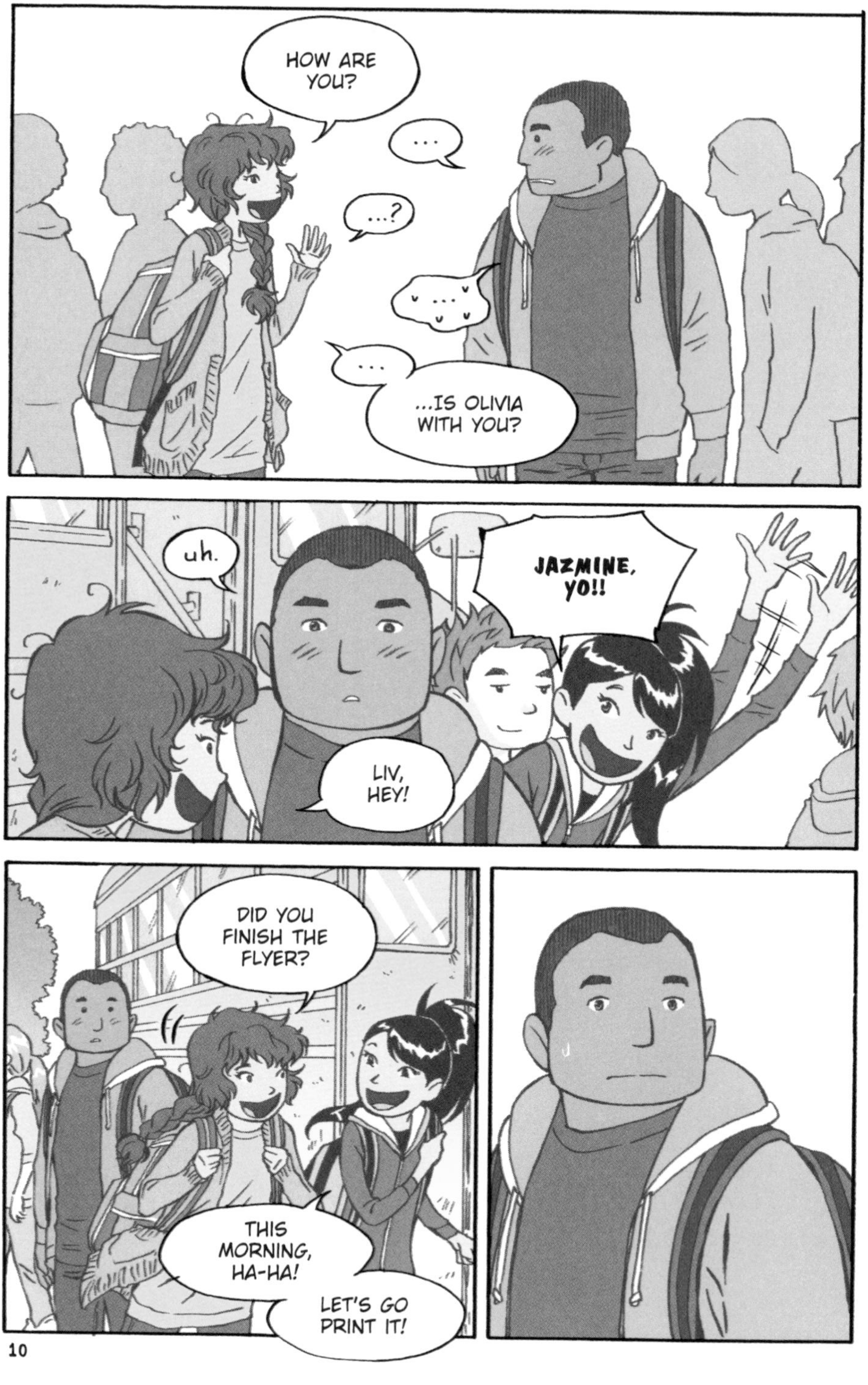
HOW ARE YOU?
...
...?
...
...
...IS OLIVIA WITH YOU?
uh.
JAZMINE, YO!!
LIV, HEY!
DID YOU FINISH THE FLYER?
THIS MORNING, HA-HA!
LET'S GO PRINT IT!

...YOU DIDN'T SEE THAT.

SCHOOL'S THE SAME OLD STUFF EVERY DAY.

TINY LOCKERS...

TINY DESKS...

WISHING YOU WERE **NOT** IN SCIENCE CLASS, TAKING A TEST...

Z

WISHING YOU WERE NOT IN CLASS, **PERIOD**.

AND THEN...

...THE HALLWAYS.

YAMMER HA HA

CHATTER

HA HA

I'M TELLING YOU, THE TRASH CANS ARE AVERAGE STUDENT-SIZED!

WHICH I HAVE TO PATROL **DAILY**...

...BECAUSE THERE'S ALWAYS SOME BEATDOWN ABOUT TO HAPPEN.

PETER'LL PROVE IT!

wha?3

HA HA HA

C-COME ON, GUYS, STOP IT!

...PRETTY SURE I HEARD HIM SAY, "STOP IT."

uh, let's go.

SOMETIMES, I DON'T EVEN HAVE TO SAY ANYTHING ANYMORE.

PEOPLE KNOW WHAT I'M ABOUT.

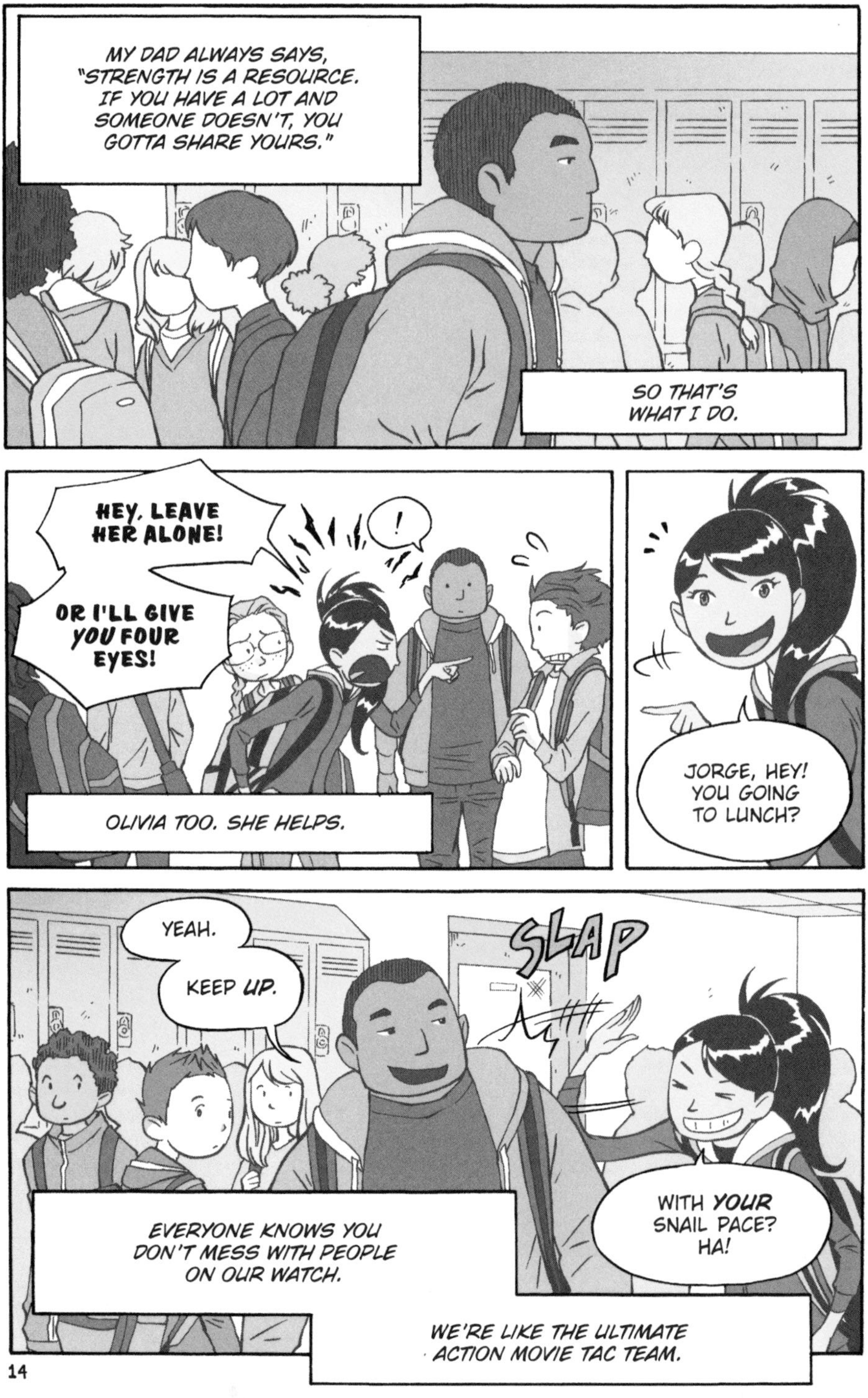
MY DAD ALWAYS SAYS, "STRENGTH IS A RESOURCE. IF YOU HAVE A LOT AND SOMEONE DOESN'T, YOU GOTTA SHARE YOURS."
SO THAT'S WHAT I DO.
HEY, LEAVE HER ALONE!
OR I'LL GIVE *YOU* FOUR EYES!
!
OLIVIA TOO. SHE HELPS.
JORGE, HEY! YOU GOING TO LUNCH?
YEAH.
KEEP *UP*.
SLAP
WITH *YOUR* SNAIL PACE? HA!
EVERYONE KNOWS YOU DON'T MESS WITH PEOPLE ON OUR WATCH.
WE'RE LIKE THE ULTIMATE ACTION MOVIE TAC TEAM.

CHRIS, HEY! WHAT'S UP?

WE'VE GOT OUR MISSION, AND NOTHING CAN STOP—

HI, JORGE!

. . .

?

. . .

. . .

...OH!

LIV, HEY! THERE YOU ARE!

HA HA HA

. . .

. . .

. . .

...WHAT IS THIS?

JORGE, HEY!

YOU GUYS GET FOOD YET?

GARRETT, YOU ALREADY MET.

HEY, SHRIMP-MAN. NOT YET. WE'RE 'BOUT TO.

HA

AND THEN, THERE'RE THE REST OF THE ATHLETICS CLUB PEOPLE.

—MOSTLY FOOLS WHO JUST WANNA KICK A BALL AROUND AND FART...

HA HA HA

JAMES, YOU GOTTA SEE THIS!

...EXCEPT FOR JAMES.

QUARTERBACK, TEAM CAPTAIN, AN HONOR STUDENT...

...AND THE MAN GARRETT WANTS TO BE WHEN HE GROWS UP.

OMG, JAMES!

HEY, MAN!

WANNA COME SIT WITH US?

GARRETT WAS QUARTERBACK AT HIS OLD SCHOOL AND REALLY, **REALLY** WANTS PROPS FROM JAMES FOR THAT.

. . .

UH.

NAW, WE GOT A TABLE ALREADY.

SORRY.

ME, I'M NOT A FAN OF THIS GUY, SO I TRY TO STEER CLEAR.

. . .

HEY, SHERIFF.

UH, HEY.

YOU'LL ASK? REALLY?

YEAH, FOR SURE!

THANKS SO MU—

HEY, ATHLETICS PEEPS!

LISTEN UP!

w-wait, right now?!

THIS IS MY FRIEND JAZMINE DUONG FROM THE DRAMA CLUB.

o-oh, right now...

um, h-hi—

THEY NEED TO MOVE SOME HEAVY STUFF TOMORROW...

...AND SHE NOTICED HOW SOME OF YOU HAVE MORE MUSCLES THAN BRAINS—

OMG I DID NOT SAY THAT!!

MPF!

S-SORRY.

IT'S JUST... THERE'S GOING TO BE A LOT OF BOXES...AND WE NEED MORE PEOPLE...

C-CAN ANY OF YOU HELP?

IT'S JUST FOR AN HOUR TOMORROW AFTER SCHOOL...

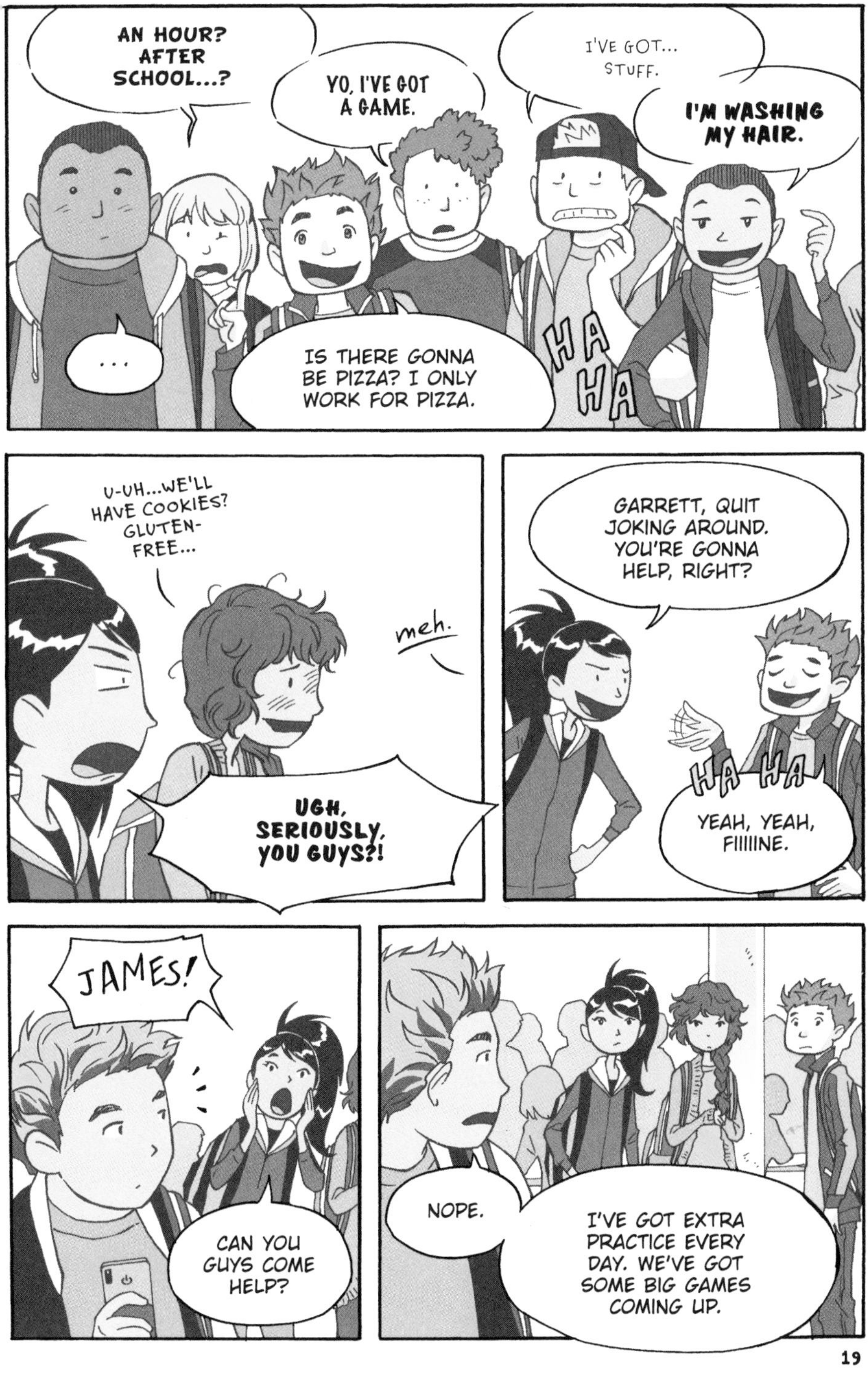
AN HOUR? AFTER SCHOOL...?
YO, I'VE GOT A GAME.
I'VE GOT... STUFF.
I'M WASHING MY HAIR.
...
IS THERE GONNA BE PIZZA? I ONLY WORK FOR PIZZA.
HA HA
U-UH...WE'LL HAVE COOKIES? GLUTEN-FREE...
meh.
UGH, SERIOUSLY, YOU GUYS?!
GARRETT, QUIT JOKING AROUND. YOU'RE GONNA HELP, RIGHT?
HA HA
YEAH, YEAH, FIIIIINE.
JAMES!
CAN YOU GUYS COME HELP?
NOPE.
I'VE GOT EXTRA PRACTICE EVERY DAY. WE'VE GOT SOME BIG GAMES COMING UP.

...

UHH, ACTUALLY...

...I JUST REMEMBERED I GOT EXTRA PRACTICE TOO.

SO I CAN'T.

WHAAAT?!

COME ON!

JORGE, YOU? YOU WON'T BAIL, RIGHT?

...

HUH? NO, I'LL COME HELP.

...YEEAAAH!!! THANKS, BUDDY!

!!

...REALLY?!

THANKS SO MUCH, JORGE!!

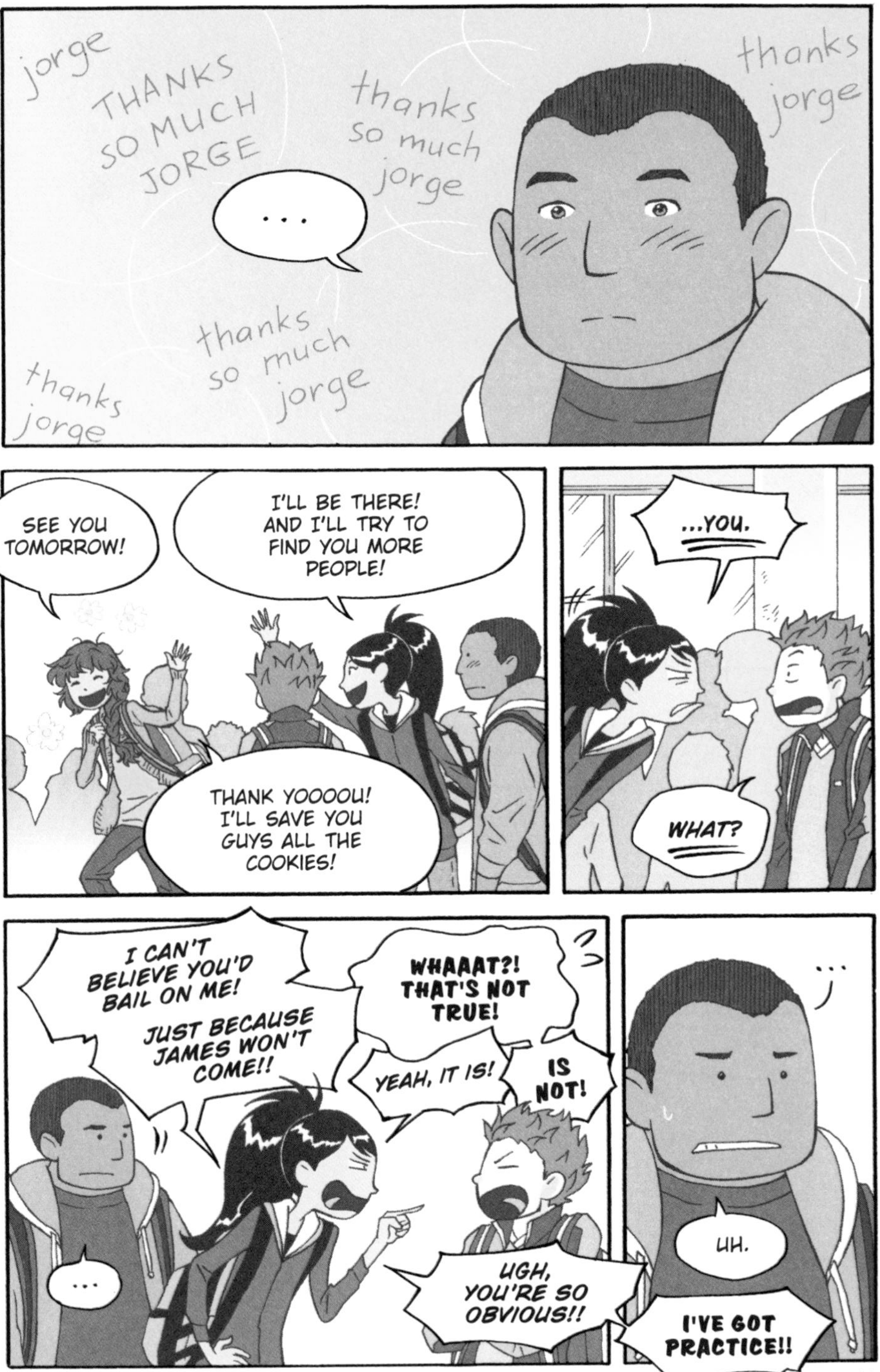
jorge
THANKS SO MUCH JORGE
thanks so much jorge
thanks jorge
. . .
thanks so much jorge
thanks jorge
SEE YOU TOMORROW!
I'LL BE THERE! AND I'LL TRY TO FIND YOU MORE PEOPLE!
THANK YOOOOU! I'LL SAVE YOU GUYS ALL THE COOKIES!
...YOU.
WHAT?
I CAN'T BELIEVE YOU'D BAIL ON ME!
JUST BECAUSE JAMES WON'T COME!!
WHAAAT?! THAT'S NOT TRUE!
YEAH, IT IS!
IS NOT!
...
UGH, YOU'RE SO OBVIOUS!!
...
UH.
I'VE GOT PRACTICE!!

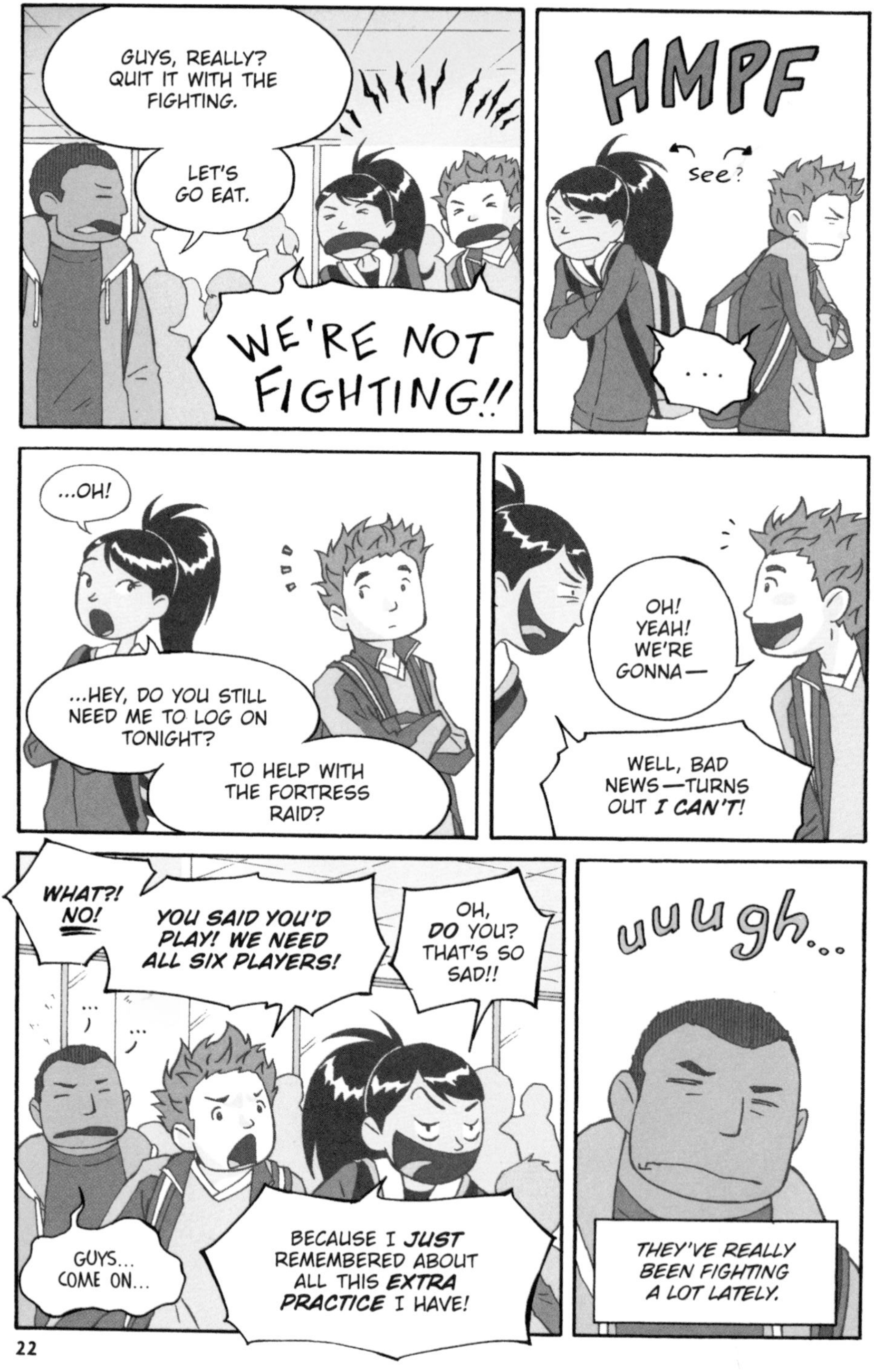
GUYS, REALLY? QUIT IT WITH THE FIGHTING.
LET'S GO EAT.
WE'RE NOT FIGHTING!!
HMPF
see?
...
...OH!
...HEY, DO YOU STILL NEED ME TO LOG ON TONIGHT?
TO HELP WITH THE FORTRESS RAID?
OH! YEAH! WE'RE GONNA—
WELL, BAD NEWS—TURNS OUT I CAN'T!
WHAT?! NO!
YOU SAID YOU'D PLAY! WE NEED ALL SIX PLAYERS!
OH, DO YOU? THAT'S SO SAD!!
BECAUSE I JUST REMEMBERED ABOUT ALL THIS EXTRA PRACTICE I HAVE!
GUYS... COME ON...
uuugh...
THEY'VE REALLY BEEN FIGHTING A LOT LATELY.

THE NEXT DAY.

HALLWAY GOSSIP THINKS THAT FIGHTING A LOT MEANS THEY'RE ABOUT TO DATE.

MURMUR WHISPER

NOD NOD

BICKER

ARGUE

...

I GIVE THEM TWO WEEKS, TOPS.

...I DON'T KNOW HOW THAT WOULD WORK, THOUGH, SINCE SHE ALREADY HAS A BOYFRIEND.

MARCUS! HIIII! ♡

COME EAT LUNCH WITH US!

IT'S REEEEEAL WEIRD FOR EVERYBODY.

...

...

OLIVIA'S EX-BOYFRIEND ↓

WE ALL JUST SORT OF DEAL WITH IT...
...EXCEPT GARRETT, WHO **REALLY** CAN'T WITH THIS, APPARENTLY.

OPEN WIDE! ♡

...

EW

UGH, I <u>CAN'T</u> WITH THIS!!

GET A <u>ROOM</u>, YOU TWO!

is it over yet? can i look?

DON'T LISTEN TO GARRETT. HE'S JUST JEALOUS.

WHAT?

SO WHAT GAME DO YOU WANNA PLAY FOR DATE NIGHT? ♡

UGH, GROSSS.

∪ ...... ∪

CHEW CHEW

...LIKE I SAID, REEEAL WEIRD FOR EVERYBODY.

I'M SO GLAD I DON'T HAVE TO WORRY ABOUT ANY OF THIS DATING NONSENSE.

WHAT A PA—

...

THANKS SO MUCH, JORGE!!

...

NO.

WHAT. IS. THIS?

# CHAPTER 2

I DO **NOT** HAVE A CRUSH ON JAZMINE.

THAT'S **STUPID**.

SHE'S NOT EVEN IN MY CLUB OR ANYTHING.

AND DATING IS **STUPID**.

YEAH.

SEE YOU TOMORROW!

BYE!

HEY, DON'T YOU GUYS HAVE ART CLUB TODAY?

HA HA

I'LL JUST GO, HELP OUT, *AND* **LEAVE**, LIKE ALL'S NORMAL.

JORGE, HEY!

DON'T GO HOME YET!

WE'RE GONNA PLAY SOME KICK-BALL! COME ON!

YO, I'M HELPING OLIVIA AT THE DRAMA THING, REMEMBER?

...AND DIDN'T YOU SAY YOU HAD HOMEWORK?

UHHH... YES?

HOMEWORK, YES!

KICKBALL... HOMEWORK?

*SNORT* UH-HUH.

DUDE, CAN YOU COVER FOR ME? LIV WILL KILL ME IF SHE FINDS OUT.

YEAH, YEAH, GO.

YEAAAH!

GOOD LUCK WITH DRAMA-LLAMAS! SEE YOU TOMORROW!

...WHAT'S HIS PROBLEM WITH THE DRAMA CLUB?

LIV'S FRIENDS WITH THEM, SO THEY CAN'T BE SO BAD.

...WAIT.

FOCUS.

GONNA GO THERE, HELP OUT ALL NORMAL—

AND **NOT** GET ALL WEIRD OVER A GIRL.

DRAMA ROOM

HA HA

NOT GONNA GET *ME.*

...HELLO?

UH.

'SUP.

HEARD YOU GUYS NEED HELP TO MOVE STUFF?

...

OH!

ARE YOU JORGE?

HA-HA, OMG, HE LOOKS JUST LIKE JAZMINE SAID!

...

?

SHE SAID, "A THOUSAND FEET TALL, LOOKS LIKE HE SHOULD HAVE HIS OWN ACTION MOVIE."

....!

WHAT?

OH! HERE SHE COMES NOW!

JAZMINE!

HEY, JAZMINE! GUESS WHO I—

OUT OF THE WAY, OUT OF THE WAY!

THE BOX IS GONNA—

RRIP

NOOOO! I ALMOST MADE IT!

IT'S OKAY, IT'S OKAY!

I DON'T THINK ANYTHING BROKE!

BEAM

JORGE! YOU DID COME!

....!

HIIIIII!

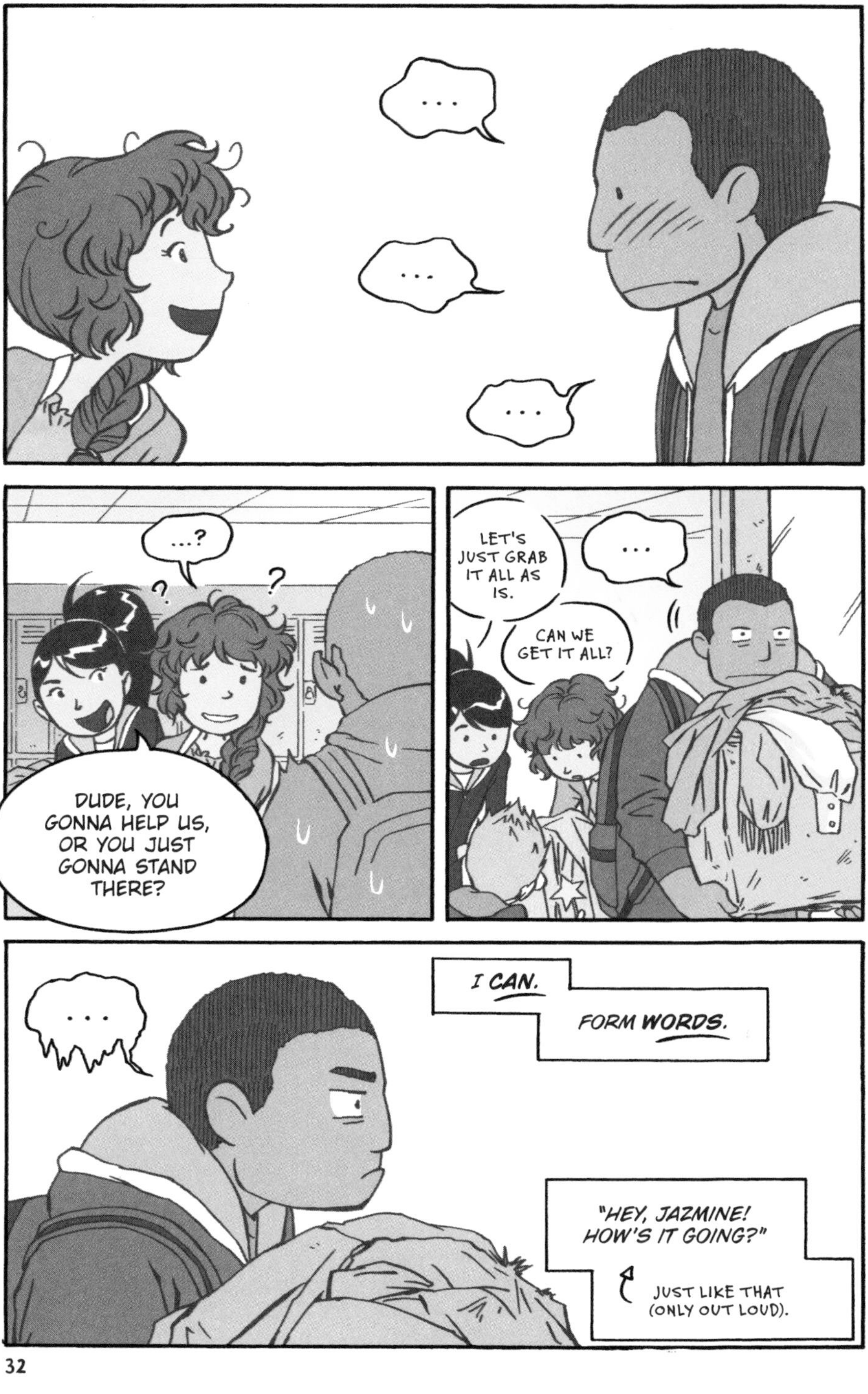
...
...
...
...?
DUDE, YOU GONNA HELP US, OR YOU JUST GONNA STAND THERE?
LET'S JUST GRAB IT ALL AS IS.
...
CAN WE GET IT ALL?
...
I CAN.
FORM WORDS.
"HEY, JAZMINE! HOW'S IT GOING?"
JUST LIKE THAT (ONLY OUT LOUD).

UH.

HA HA

PILE IT HIGH!

WHERE DOES THAT GO?

MRS. FERRIS! THIS ONE'S ALL RIPPED!

DO I...

...JUST DROP IT ANYWHERE?

OH MY GOSH, YOU MUST BE JORGE!

YOU LOOK JUST LIKE...

...JAZMINE DESCRIBED YOU!

...

I'M MRS. FERRIS, THE NEW DRAMA TEACHER.

O-OKAY.

YOU CAN JUST PUT THE BOXES IN MY OFFICE. HERE!

33

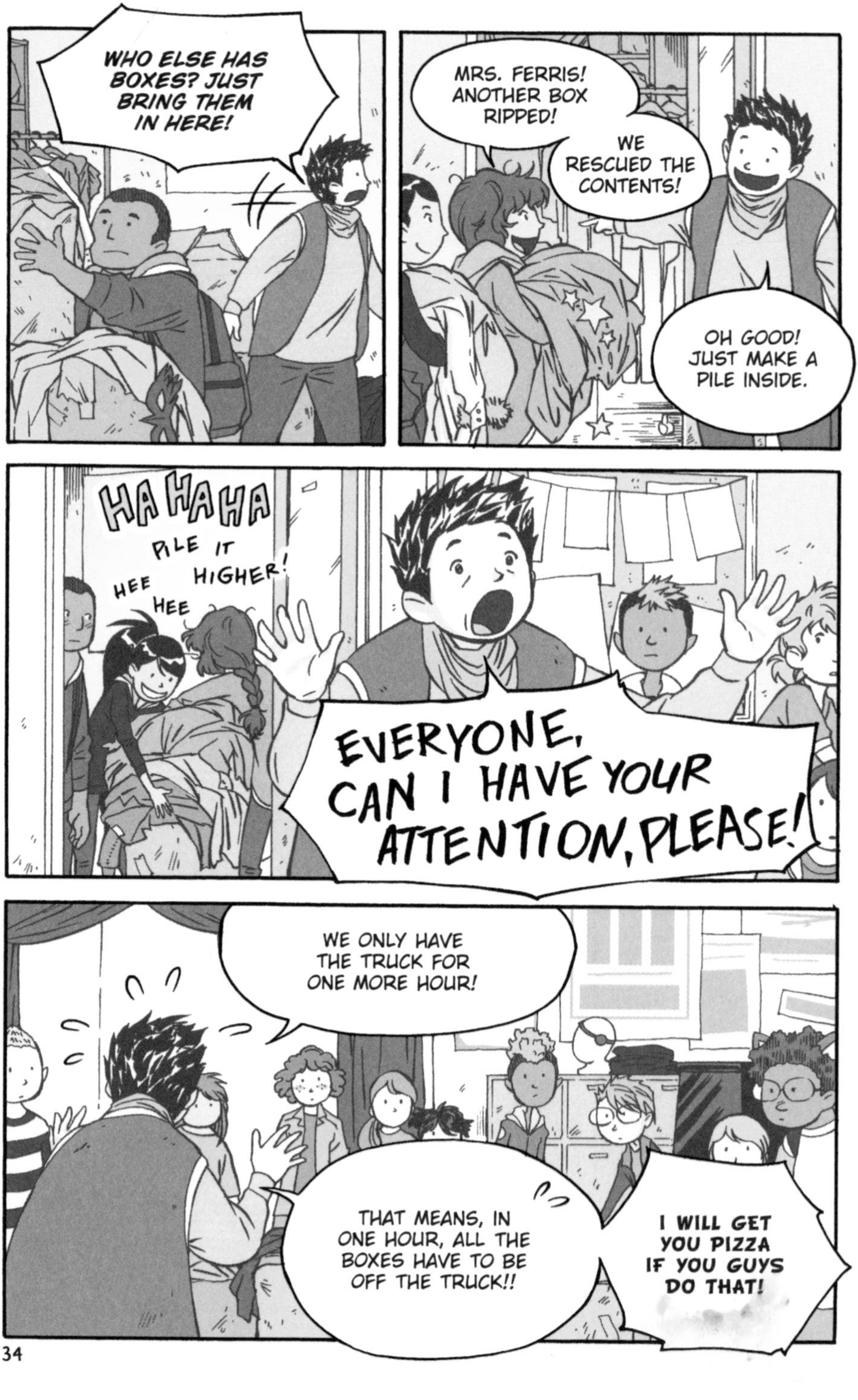
WHO ELSE HAS BOXES? JUST BRING THEM IN HERE!
MRS. FERRIS! ANOTHER BOX RIPPED!
WE RESCUED THE CONTENTS!
OH GOOD! JUST MAKE A PILE INSIDE.
HA HA HA HA
PILE IT HIGHER!
HEE HEE
EVERYONE, CAN I HAVE YOUR ATTENTION, PLEASE!
WE ONLY HAVE THE TRUCK FOR ONE MORE HOUR!
THAT MEANS, IN ONE HOUR, ALL THE BOXES HAVE TO BE OFF THE TRUCK!!
I WILL GET YOU PIZZA IF YOU GUYS DO THAT!

ALL THE PIZZA.

pizza?

...UHHH...JUST AN *HOUR?*

THERE ARE A LOT OF BOXES...

SOUNDS LIKE A *CHALLENGE.*

HEY, JORGE.

BET I CAN MOVE MORE BOXES THAN YOU.

WHAT? HEY, WAIT.

DASH

GO GO GO

ARE WE REALLY GONNA GET PIZZA?

...WHOA!

....!

...SHE WASN'T KIDDING ABOUT THE BOXES!

...ON YOUR LEFT! -ᴗ-

!

GIVE ME THREE BOXES.

UH, THE LIMIT'S ONE, KID, SORRY...

OR IT'LL BE TOO HEAVY.

MORE BOXES INCO—

NIC, NO!

STACK THEM BY THE WALL!

SCUFFLE YAMMER CHA

DON'T JUST DROP THEM RANDOMLY. SOMEONE'LL TRIP OVER THAT!

JASON!

STACKS SHOULD BE FOUR BOXES HIGH, OKAY?

UH, J.

HEY.

HELLO

OR THEY'LL TOPPLE!

J !!

ZEKE!!

HEY, SORRY.

WHERE DO YOU WANT THIS BOX?

OVER THERE IN THE CORNER, PLEASE!

THANK YOUUU!

...

CASUAL

'SUP, JAZMINE. GOT A BOX HERE. WHERE DO YOU WANT IT?

OVER THERE. THANK YOU, JORGE!

...OKAY.

FORM. WORDS.

CASUAL.

HEY, JAZMINE—

TURN

JORGE!

YES?

...

...

uh.

box.

where..?

OH, THE BOX!

CAN YOU PUT IT IN THE STACK OVER THERE, PLEASE?

THANK YOU!

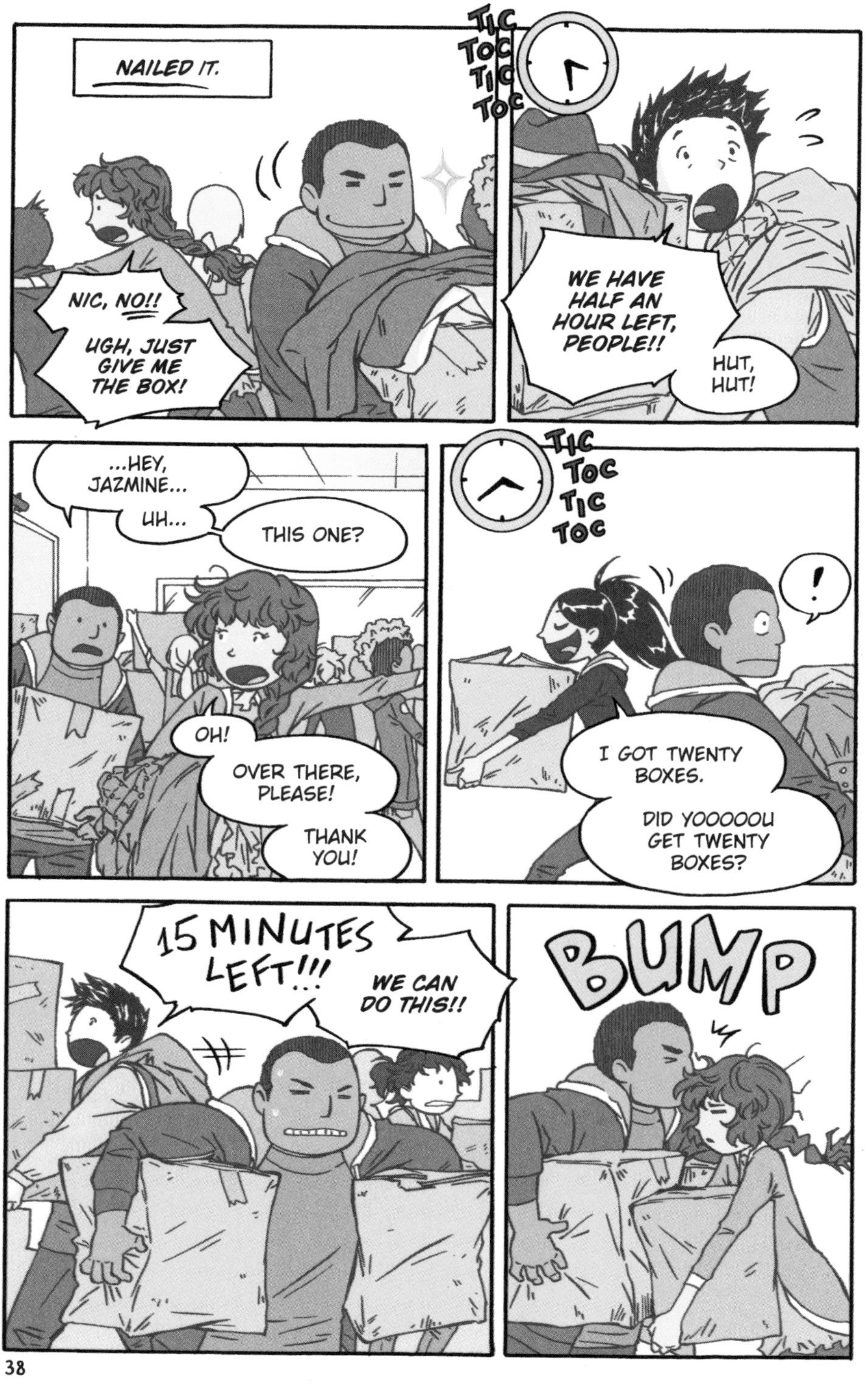
NAILED IT.
NIC, NO!!
UGH, JUST GIVE ME THE BOX!
TIC TOC TIC TOC
WE HAVE HALF AN HOUR LEFT, PEOPLE!!
HUT, HUT!
...HEY, JAZMINE...
UH...
THIS ONE?
OH!
OVER THERE, PLEASE!
THANK YOU!
TIC TOC TIC TOC
!
I GOT TWENTY BOXES.
DID YOOOOOU GET TWENTY BOXES?
15 MINUTES LEFT!!!
...
WE CAN DO THIS!!
BUMP

ACK, I'M SO SORRY!

IT'S OKAY, IT'S OKAY!

ARE YOU ALL RIGHT?

YES!

...ARE THE BOXES...?

5 MINUTES LEFT!!

TRUDGE

...THE LAST...

...TWO...

...BOXES...

STAGGER

YAAAAAK...

JUST GONNA...PUT THEM ANYWHERE...YOU CAN'T STOP ME...

WHICH ONE OF US...

WON...?

PROBABLY ME...

LIKE FUN IT WAS.

YOU GUYS ARE AMAZING!

YOU DID IT!

YOU...

UM, HELLO?

I HAVE A DELIVERY HERE FOR..."ALL THE PIZZA! ALL OF IT?"

....!

OM NOM NOM

... ... I WAS SO HUNGRY.

YOU AND ALL OF US, NIC.

I CAN'T BELIEVE WE MOVED ALL THAT!

WHAT WERE WE LUGGING ANYWAY?

COSTUMES! ♥

THE LOCAL COSTUME STORE WAS CLEARING OUT THEIR OLD STUFF.

AND MRS. FERRIS'S WIFE GOT THEM TO DONATE IT TO US!

NOW WE HAVE ALL THE COSTUMES IN THE LAND!

SCORE

YEAH!

TURN

THANKS SO MUCH FOR COMING TO HELP, YOU GUYS.

JORGE, ESPECIALLY YOU! I KNOW YOU DIDN'T HAVE TO.

UH, NO BIG.

...*AND* YOU'RE TALKING TO ME!!!

HA HA FINALLY!

I WAS STARTING TO THINK YOU HATE ME OR SOMETHING.

HEY, J...

...IS THIS SPOT TAKEN?

ZEKE!

HA-HA, YOU KNOW IT'S NOT.

...

SIT, SIT!

HA HA

'SUP.

JORGE, I DON'T KNOW IF YOU'VE MET MY BOYFRIEND, ZEKE? HE'S IN THE...

...YEARBOOK CLUB AND...

STAND

....!

DUDE, YOU OKAY?

?

I HAVE TO GO.

what? but pizza!

I FORGOT.

I HAVE A...

HAVE A THING.

GOTTA GO... DO IT.

OH, OKAY. SEE YOU TOMORROW!

BYE, JORGE!

THANKS AGAIN!

WHAT IS THIS?

I SUDDENLY **REALLY** HAD TO GET OUT OF THERE.

...DO I...LIKE JAZMINE?

# CHAPTER 3

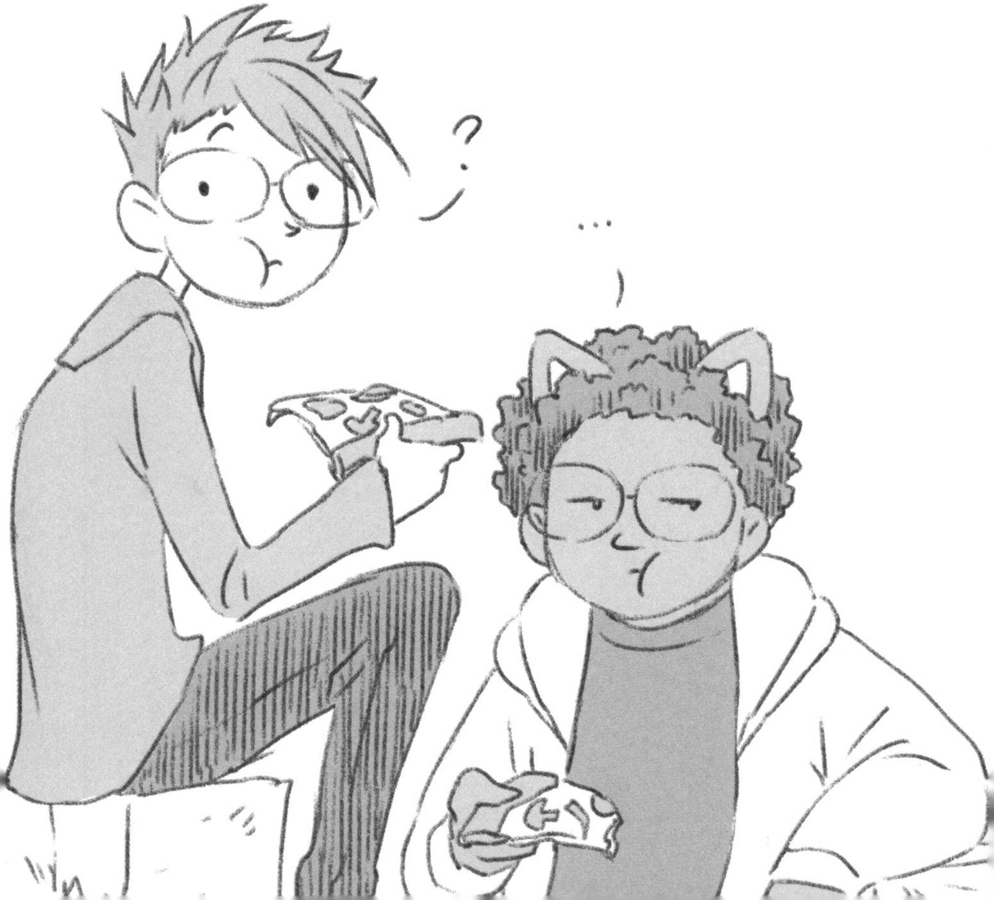
?
...

NEXT DAY.

JORGE, HEADS UP!

RRING

WACK

MAN, WHAT'S UP WITH YOU?!

YOU'RE REALLY OUT OF IT TODAY.

ARE YOU SICK OR SOMETHING?

TOSS

I'M *FINE!!*

WATCH WHERE YOU THROW THAT THING.

...ARE YOU REALLY OKAY?

YOU DON'T *LOOK* OKAY.

...

YOU'VE BEEN WEIRD ALL DAY.

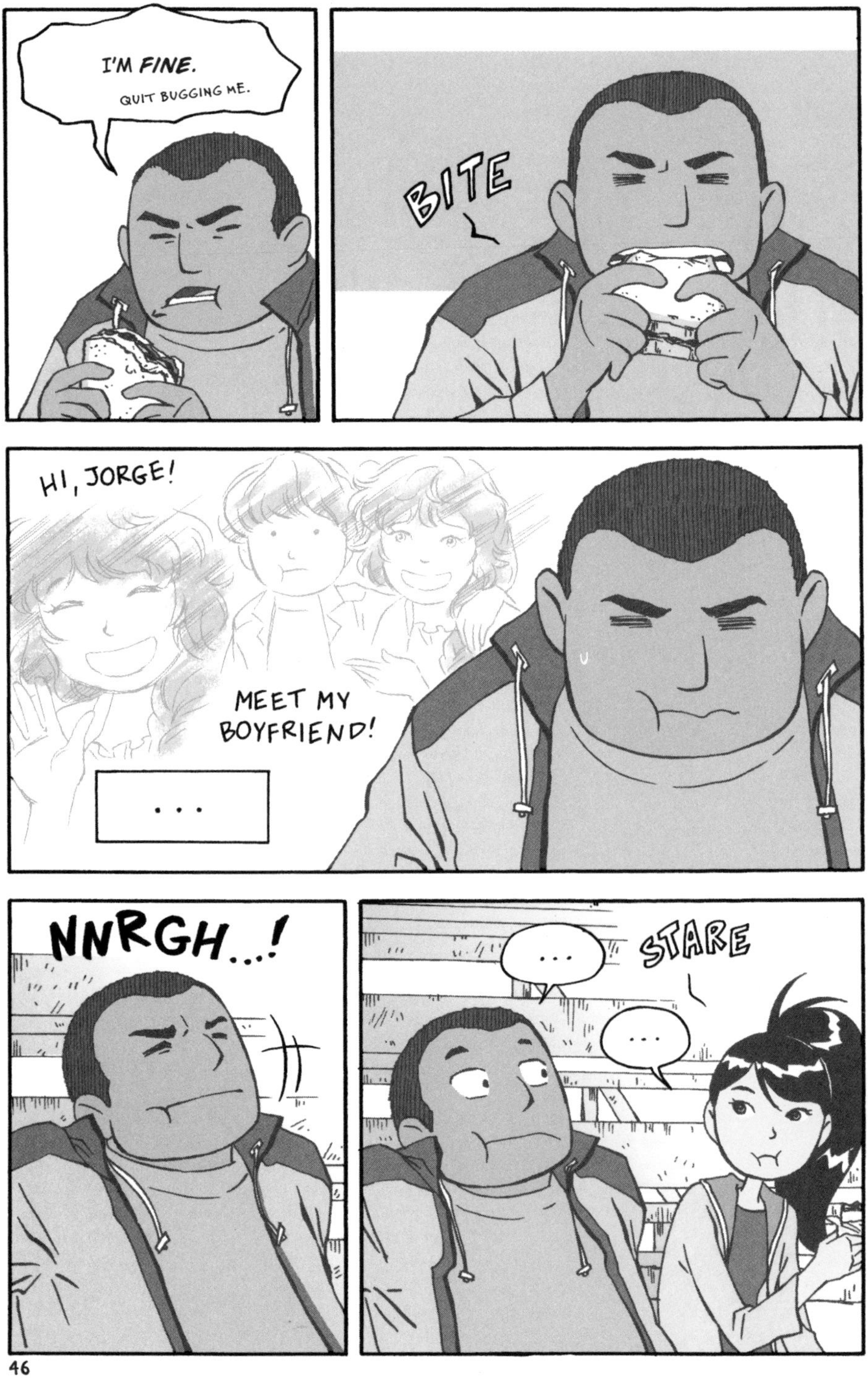
I'M FINE.
QUIT BUGGING ME.
BITE
HI, JORGE!
MEET MY BOYFRIEND!
. . .
NNRGH...!
...
STARE
...

...HEY, UH.

...YOU KNOW YOU CAN TALK TO ME, RIGHT?

ABOUT WHATEVER IT IS?

···

JUST... YOU KNOW...

UNLOAD. YOU KNOW I'LL ALWAYS LISTEN.

YEAH?

...YEAH.

GOOD.

LIV IS A GOOD FRIEND.

FWUMP!

....!

...OH. HEY, SHRIMP-MAN.

HEY.

MAN, YOU'RE *BOTH* LIKE SULKY *BABIES* TODAY.

PFFT

WHAT'S *YOUR* PROBLEM?

YOU WORRIED ABOUT THE GAME THIS WEEKEND OR SOMETHING?

HMPF.

WHY WOULD I WORRY ABOUT *THAT*?

YOU KNOW I WON'T EVEN GET TO PLAY!

SHE'S JUST GONNA KEEP ME ON THE BENCH *FOREVER*.

WHILE JAMES PLAYS ALL THE GAMES.

WHOA, GRUMPY.

HEY, I WAS A STARTER AT MY OLD SCHOOL! I WON GAMES!

SHRUG

I SHOULD BE STARTER QUARTERBACK, NOT JAMES!

DON'T YOU THINK I'M BETTER THAN HIM?!

HMM, JAMES IS PRETTY GOOD, THOUGH.

YEAH.

UGH, SOME FRIENDS YOU ARE.

WANNA QUIT FOOTBALL AND COME PLAY BASEBALL WITH ME?

100% LESS SKULL DAMAGE.

OR DO JIU-JITSU WITH ME! 1000% MORE SKULL DAMAGE, I PROMISE.

I WILL PERSONALLY DO IT.

RR STL

HA-HA, WHAT?! NO, YOU GOONS.

...WHY'RE YOU ALL SOUR ABOUT IT ALL OF A SUDDEN?

YEAH, DUDE, YOU'VE BEEN BACKUP FOR WEEKS. WHAT CHANGED?

...

mumble

mumble

HUH?

WHAT?

I'M NOT PART OF THE TEAM, OKAY? NOT REALLY.

THAT'S WHAT IT FEELS LIKE.

NO MATTER HOW HARD I TRY.

49

WHAT? BUT YOU GUYS ARE ALWAYS HANGING OUT TOGETHER! LAUGHING AND—

NOT WITH *JAMES* AND *HIS* CREW.

THEY JUST IGNORE ME.

...OH.

...AND ALSO...

UH...

...MY MOM WANTS TO THROW A TEAM "BONDING" PARTY...

...AND WAS ALL, "JUST INVITE THEM ALL!"

AND I'M LIKE...

...WILL THEY EVEN SHOW UP...?

JAMES AND THEM?

...

JAMES, HUH?

YOUR PARTY? HE'LL BE THERE.

GIVE ME A FEW DAYS.

RRRING

SHE'LL MAKE IT HAPPEN. LIV'S SOCIAL KNOW-HOW IS LIKE A SUPERPOWER.

SLAM

IF SHE EVER TURNED EVIL, WE'D ALL BE IN TROUBLE.

—!

OW, STOP IT!

NICE HAIR!

HA HA HA

ZEKE.

51

...AND JAMES.

HEY, BIG GUY. CAN WE COUNT ON YOU FOR BETTER YEARBOOK PHOTOS THIS YEAR?

C'MON, YOU'LL BE A PAL, RIGHT?

MAYBE IF YOU GET *BETTER FACES.*

LIKE, WITH *INTELLIGENCE.*

OOOOH, FIGHTING WORDS!

HA HA HA

MUSS MUSS

LEMME GO...!!

....!

WHAT'S GOING ON HERE?

UH-OH, THE SHERIFF'S HERE!

HA HA let him go.

WE WERE JUST PLAYIN'. DON'T WORRY.

NO HARM, NO FOUL.

SEE YOU AT THE ATHLETICS CLUB MEET AFTER SCHOOL, YEAH?

SLAP

…

HA HA HA

…HEY, UH, ZEKE, RIGHT?

ARE YOU OKA—

LEAVE ME ALONE!!

ALL YOU BRAINLESS NEANDERTHALS SHOULD STAY AWAY FROM CIVILIZED PEOPLE!

…WHAAA…?

…

EVERY DAY, LIFE MAKES LESS AND LESS SENSE.

FWEET

...THIS IS WHY I LOVE SPORTS.

RULES ARE CLEAR.

BOUNCE

AWW!!

ALMOST!!

(UNLIKE MIDDLE SCHOOL LIFE, UGH.)

YOU EITHER DON'T MAKE THAT SHOT—

OR YOU DO.

THUK

YEAAAH!!

FEELS LIKE A MILLION BUCKS.

(...I ASSUME. I'VE NEVER SEEN A MILLION BUCKS.)

MAN, WISH I HAD YOU ON THE TEAM!

HA HA

STOP COURTING HIM! YOU KNOW HE'S IN LOVE WITH BASEBALL!

HA HA

IT'S TRUE. BASEBALL IS BASICALLY THE BEST.

*FIGHT ME.*

YOU COMING TO THE ATHLETICS MEET TODAY?

YEP.

GOOD.

FOOTBALL TEAM WANTS ALL THE BUDGET APPARENTLY. AGAIN.

MIGHT BE A FIIIIGHT.

*SNORT*

RRING

ATHLETICS CLUB MEETS ARE *ALWAYS* A FIGHT.

YAMMER

YO, DID YOUR MOM PICK YOUR SHIRT?

YEAH...MY MOM ACTUALLY *CARES* HOW I LOOK.

OOOOOH!

HA HA BURN!

CHATTER BICKER

EVERYTHING'S A SHOWDOWN, TRYING TO ONE-UP EACH OTHER, EVEN WITH TALKING.

COACH RASHAD IS *WAAAY* NOT INTO THAT, THOUGH.

FWEEET

*SETTLE DOWN, OR IT'S FIFTY LAPS FOR ALL OF YOU!*

HA HA HA TAG!!

AND NO ONE WILL MESS WITH HER BECAUSE RUMOR IS SHE CAN BENCH-PRESS A *TRUCK.*

OKAY, BEFORE WE START—THIS IS YOUR MONTHLY REMINDER. TRASH TALK?

*STILL NOT ALLOWED* ON SCHOOL TEAMS.

IF YOU CAN'T USE YOUR SPORTS SKILLS TO WIN AND HAVE TO RESORT TO VERBAL ABUSE AND INSULTS ON MY FIELD—

—HA HA

—GET OFF MY FIELD.

....!

JAMES.

MOVING ON—

ATHLETIC FUND-RAISER BALL IS IN SEVEN WEEKS. THERE'S A LOT TO DO.

ARE ALL THE TEAM REPS HERE?

YEP!

HERE.

*GOOD.*

TICKETS, PEOPLE!

WE NEED TO **SELL MORE TICKETS!**

REMEMBER— THE MORE MONEY WE RAISE, THE MORE STUFF WE CAN AFFORD FOR THE TEAMS!

FAMILY, FRIENDS, ENEMIES— EVERYONE'S FAIR GAME.

SO PUT YOUR HEADS TOGETHER AND FIGURE OUT A STRATEGY.

GO.

YEAH!

CHATTER

OMG, LIV, WEREN'T WE JUST TALKING ABOUT THIS?!!

SPIRIT SQUAD IS *SO* HERE FOR THIS!!

YES!! TEAM UP!!

HEY!

WE COULD DO, LIKE, A WHOLE EVENT IN THE CAFETERIA AND—

...

YEAH, YEAH, GOOD. UH...

...HOW ABOUT STARTING WITH THE FOOTBALL GUYS?

THEY GOT THE MOST PEOPLE.

OMG, YES!!

I'LL GO ASK!

JAMES?

HEY, GUYS!

H-HEY, BROOKE.

I'VE GOT AN AWESOME IDEA!!

...

...

~~~~ !!

DON'T YOU THINK JAMES WILL SHOW UP AT GARRETT'S PARTY...

HEH HEH HEH

...IF *BROOKE* WAS THERE?

!

OH!

HA-HA, YEAH.

YEP. IF LIV EVER WEAPONIZED HER SOCIAL SKILLS, WE'D ALL BE DOOMED.

SEE YOU TOMORROW, JORGE!

I'M GOING OVER TO BROOKE'S HOUSE.

SEE YA!

... 

PHEW. LONG DAY TODAY.

STILL GOT HOMEWORK AND BASEBALL PRACTI—

PSST! JORGE...

....!

PUSH

I'm doing it...

I'm doing it!

...ZEKE? WHAT—?

...ARE JAMES AND THE OTHERS GONE...?

UH, YEAH, THEY LEFT A WHILE AGO.

WHAT...?

LISTEN, UH...

I JUST WANTED TO SAY...

...!

S-SORRY FOR YELLING AT YOU TODAY.

I DIDN'T MEAN IT.

There. Happy?

yaaay!

HI, JORGE!

SORRY HE BLEW UP AT YOU LIKE THAT.

HE WAS JUST... SCARED AND UPSET, Y'KNOW?

ABOUT JAMES AND THEM.

WE KNOW YOU'RE A GOOD GUY.

...

UH.

IT'S COOL.

DON'T WORRY ABOUT IT.

See? I told you he's awesome.

...

ANYWAY, SORRY FOR STALKING YOU...

I KNOW YOU AND LIV HAD CLUB MEET TODAY.

WE'LL GO NOW.

BYE!

THANKS SO MUCH FOR LOOKING OUT FOR EVERYONE!

BYYYE!

...

BYE.

...

# CHAPTER 4

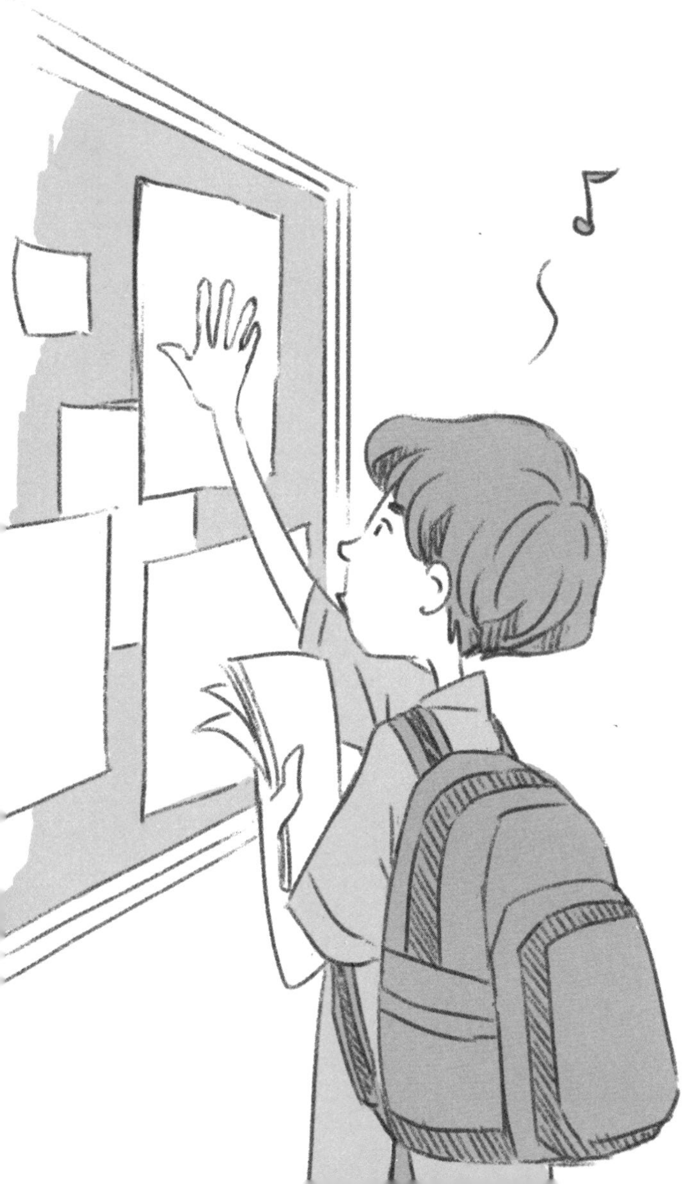

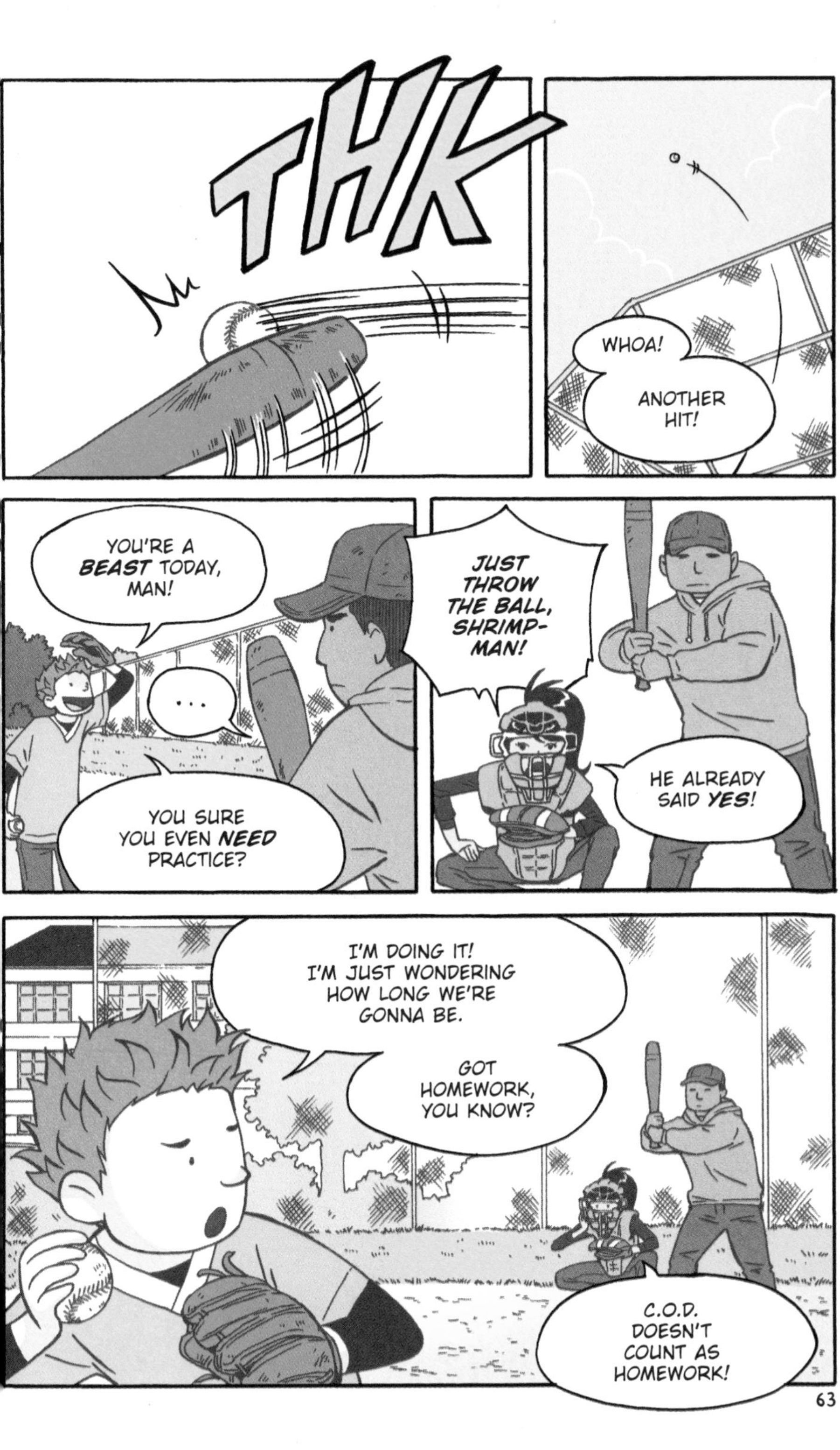
THK
WHOA!
ANOTHER HIT!
YOU'RE A BEAST TODAY, MAN!
...
YOU SURE YOU EVEN NEED PRACTICE?
JUST THROW THE BALL, SHRIMP-MAN!
HE ALREADY SAID YES!
I'M DOING IT! I'M JUST WONDERING HOW LONG WE'RE GONNA BE.
GOT HOMEWORK, YOU KNOW?
C.O.D. DOESN'T COUNT AS HOMEWORK!

ACTUALLY, IT'S MADDEN.

I *KNEW* IT! HA HA

UGH.

PITCH ALREADY, DUDE!!

THK

...SO YOU REALLY THINK YOU CAN GET JAMES TO COME TO MY PARTY?

...

OH, HE'S COMING. DON'T WORRY.

YOU'RE THE BEST!

BEAM

COME ON, YOU KNOW I'VE GOT YOUR BACK.

...UNLESS YOU'RE POOPING IN OLD MAN DAN'S BUSHES AGAIN.

UGH!!

I'M NOT COVERING FOR *THAT* AGAIN!

OH MY GOD, I WAS SIX!!!

ARE YOU EVER GONNA LET THAT GO?!!

NOPE.

HA HA HA

HEY, BIG J AND I WERE SIX TOO!

...

YOU DIDN'T SEE US POOPING IN HIS BUSHES. RIGHT, J?

...J?

...

....!

PEER

HELLO?

OH!

UH, YEAH.

SURE.

YOU OKAY? YOU'VE BEEN SO QUIET.

I'M FINE.

...HEY, REMEMBER THAT TIME WE PUT UP A TENT IN LIV'S BACKYARD?

HA HA

...AND FOLDED IT RIGHT ON TOP OF HER?

I THOUGHT SHE WAS GONNA MURDER US.

UGH, I SHOULD'VE!!!

RRRING

I'M NOT FINE.

I NOTICE HER **EVERYWHERE** NOW.

HA HA HA

DUDE...?!

SOMETIMES, SHE NOTICES ME.

OH, HI, JORGE!

HOW ARE YOU?

H-HEY.

...

AND THERE'S A SCENT, LIKE, HER SHAMPOO OR SOMETHING?

AAARGH.

...

...HEY, IS IT HARD TO TRANSFER TO ANOTHER SCHOOL?

...HUH? WHY?

DON'T DO IT, MAN!! WE NEED YOU!

OR AT LEAST WAIT UNTIL THE SEASON'S OVER.

HA HA

OKAY, SHUT UP, EVERYONE. I HAVE GOOD NEWS!

OH, DID YOU BREAK UP WITH YOUR BOYFRIEND?

NO. SHUT IT, GARRETT.

WE'RE OFFICIALLY PAST 60% IN TICKET SALES FOR THE ATHLETICS BALL!!

WOO-HOO

WHOA, ALREADY?

NICE!!

WE GOTTA KEEP AT IT, OBVIOUSLY...

...SELL, LIKE, 110%...

...BUT IN THE MEANTIME!

SLIIIIDE

WHO'S GOT A DATE FOR THE BALL?!

DOES ANYONE NEED A DATE FOR THE BALL?

UUUGH!

GIVE IT A REST!

67

WHAAAAAT?

I MEAN IT!

STOPPIT WITH YOUR MATCH-MAKING SCHEMES!

WE'RE ALL JUST GONNA GO AS FRIENDS AND HAVE FUN.

RIGHT, GUYS?

YEAH!

MAYBE A LITTLE DATE, THO'? NO...?

YEAH, I'M DOWN.

YOU GUYS ARE ZERO FUN.

HMPF

HEY, NOT EVERYONE'S OBSESSED WITH DATING RANDOM NPCs LIKE YOU ARE.

GARRETT BROCK, I WILL END YOU. ☠

HEY, DON'T HATE! DON'T HATE!

SOME OF US JUST WANNA BE FREE AGENTS!

WE DON'T NEED DATES FOR ANY STUPID BALL, AMIRITE, J?

...

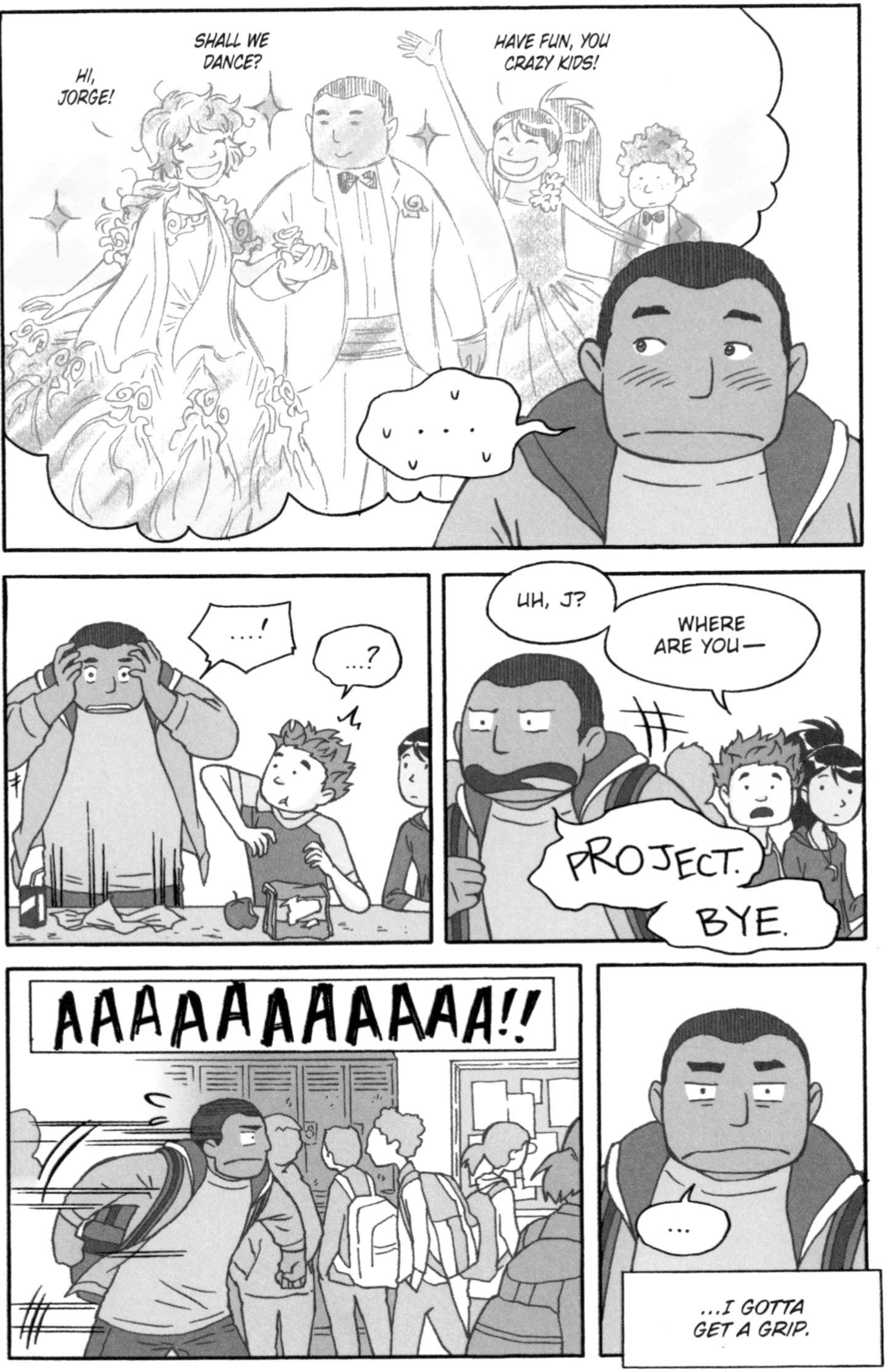
HI, JORGE!
SHALL WE DANCE?
HAVE FUN, YOU CRAZY KIDS!
. . . .
....!
...?
UH, J?
WHERE ARE YOU—
PROJECT.
BYE.
AAAAAAAAAAA!!
...
...I GOTTA GET A GRIP.

HA HA

JENNY, HEY!

CHATTER

Hi.

...

HAVEN'T EATEN LUNCH ALONE IN FOREVER.

CHEW

CHEW

...BUT AT LEAST IT'S QUIET HERE.

SIGH

JORGE?

OH, COME ON!

!!

I THOUGHT IT WAS YOU!

... UH.

HEY, ZEKE.

SIT

...!

SO, HEY!

JAZMINE TOLD YOU, RIGHT? I'M AN EDITOR WITH THE YEARBOOK CLUB?

...

YEAH?

I'M DOING THE ATHLETICS SECTION, AND I THOUGHT...

...YOU COULD HELP!

THAT WAY, I'LL GET ALL THE INFO ACCURATE...

...AND *JAMES* WON'T BUG ME.

WHAT. ARGH.

YOU CAN BE MY SOURCE *AND* MY BODYGUARD!

...

...

WE CAN DO AN INTERVIEW WITH YOU—REALLY MAKE THE ATHLETICS CLUB LOOK GOOD, YOU KNOW?

GET EVERYTHING RIGHT.

...

...IT'S GONNA HELP THE CLUB, HUH?

UH.

...SOOO...

IS THAT A YES OR A NO?

...

RRING

NEXT DAY.

HA HA

HEY!

ERRYBROOK MIDDLE SCHOOL

...OKAY, SO I SAID YES.

(...BECAUSE I MAKE BAD LIFE DECISIONS.)

JORGE, HIIIII!

I HEARD YOU WERE HELPING! THANK YOU!

I SHOULD'VE SAID NO.

I WISH...

...I DIDN'T FORGET HOW WORDS WORK WHEN SHE'S AROUND.

...AND THAT ZEKE WASN'T AROUND.

SHE LIKES HIM...SO HE MUST BE OKAY...

BUT...

HE'S **WEIRD**.

LIKE, HE'LL BE ALL NICE AND COOL ONE MINUTE—

AND THEN JUST TURN **NASTY** ON SOMETHING.

...

...JORGE?

...JORGE!

HUH?

BACK ME UP, MAN!

THEY TOTALLY SHOULD, RIGHT?

...SHOULD WHAT?

COME WITH US TO GARRETT'S PARTY!!

HALF THE TEAM REPS WILL BE THERE, SO YOU CAN REALLY TALK TO THEM!

...!

REALLY? YEAH, OKAY!

...WAIT, WHAT.

THE DAY OF GARRETT'S PARTY.

...

DING DONG

...

JORGE!! THERE YOU ARE!

YOU'RE LATE, DUDE.

MY MOM INSISTED ON COOKING. HERE.

IT'S YOUR PROBLEM NOW.

SHOVE

OOOOH, THAT SMELLS AMAZING.

MOOOOM! MRS. RUIZ SENT FOOD AGAIN!

PUT IT IN THE KITCHEN! I'LL EAT ALL OF IT!

HI, JORGE!

UGH, NO! LEAVE US SOME!!

C'MON, MAN. PARTY'S DOWNSTAIRS.

75

PARTY?

...

EVERYONE LOOKS SO BORED...

U-UH...

HEY, GUYS, MAKE SURE TO TRY ALL THESE SNACKS HERE!

...

MM.

...

THEY'RE TOTALLY IGNORING HIM...

NO WONDER HE WAS WORRIED.

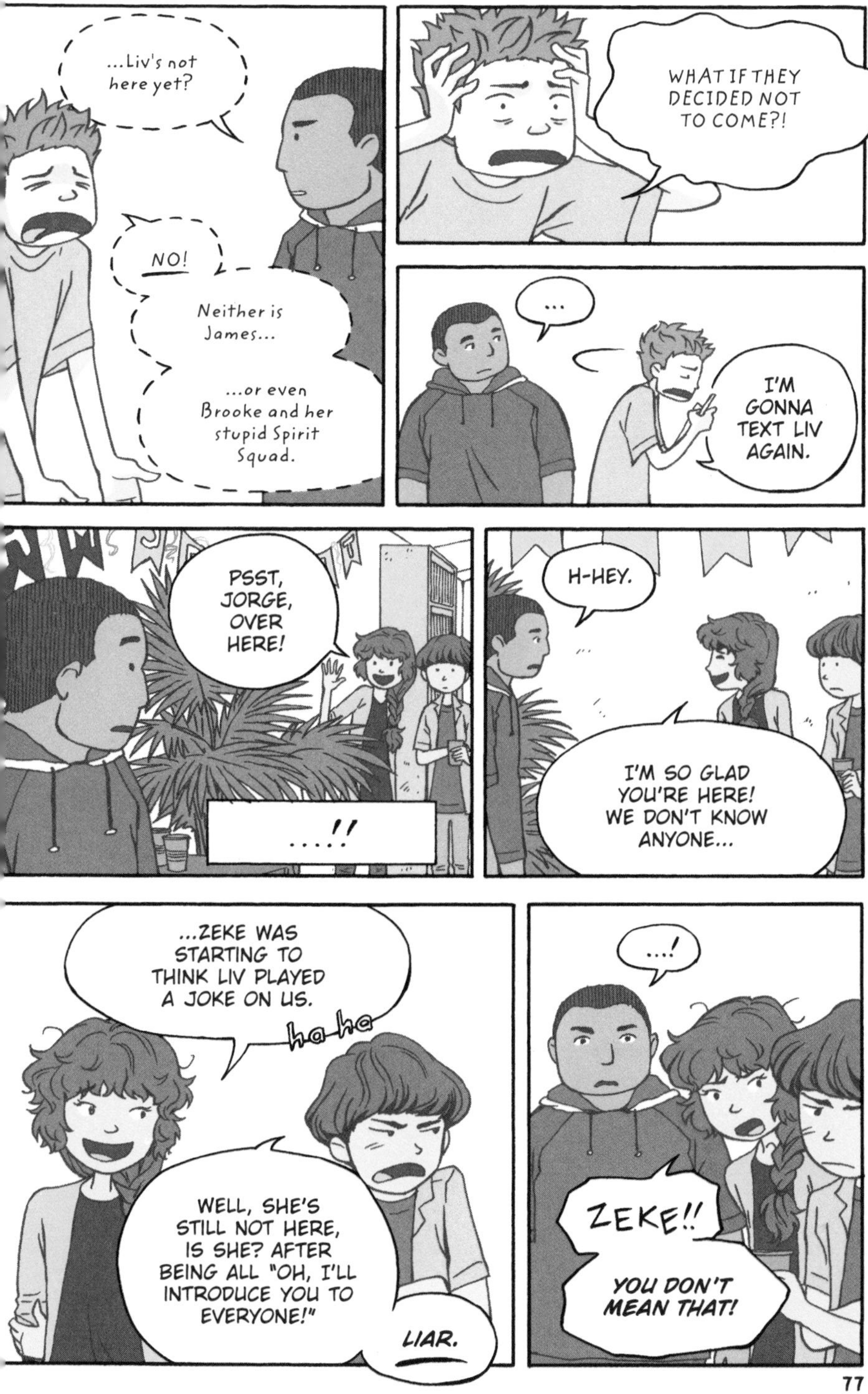

...Liv's not here yet?
NO!
Neither is James...
...or even Brooke and her stupid Spirit Squad.
WHAT IF THEY DECIDED NOT TO COME?!
...
I'M GONNA TEXT LIV AGAIN.
PSST, JORGE, OVER HERE!
....!!
H-HEY.
I'M SO GLAD YOU'RE HERE! WE DON'T KNOW ANYONE...
...ZEKE WAS STARTING TO THINK LIV PLAYED A JOKE ON US.
ha ha
WELL, SHE'S STILL NOT HERE, IS SHE? AFTER BEING ALL "OH, I'LL INTRODUCE YOU TO EVERYONE!"
LIAR.
...!
ZEKE!!
YOU DON'T MEAN THAT!

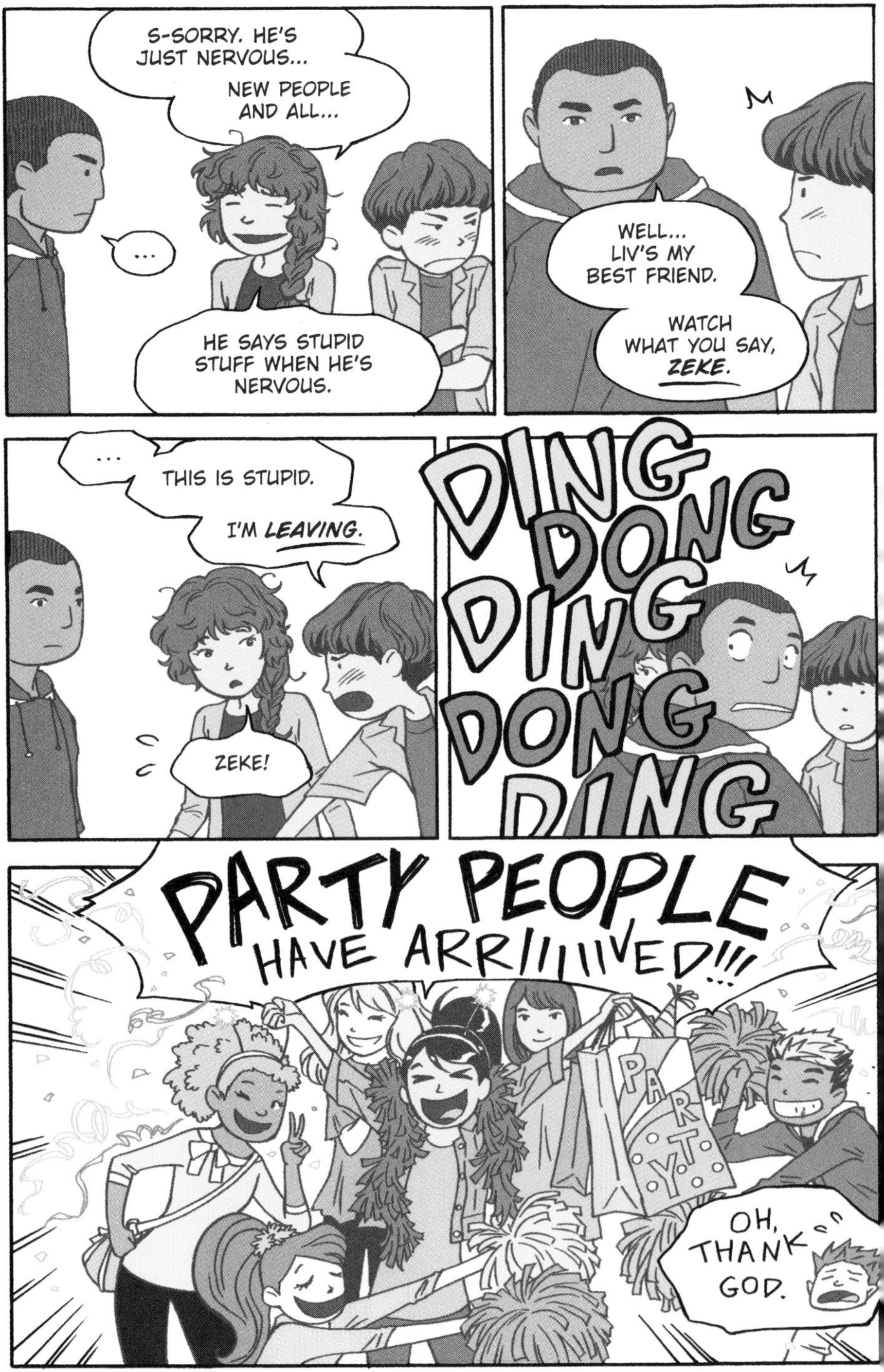
S-SORRY. HE'S JUST NERVOUS...
NEW PEOPLE AND ALL...
...
HE SAYS STUPID STUFF WHEN HE'S NERVOUS.
WELL... LIV'S MY BEST FRIEND.
WATCH WHAT YOU SAY, ZEKE.
...
THIS IS STUPID.
I'M LEAVING.
ZEKE!
DING DONG DING DONG DING
PARTY PEOPLE HAVE ARRIIIIIIVED!!!
PARTY
OH, THANK GOD.

WHERE WERE YOU GUYS?!

I TEXTED...

HA HA

HA HA

SORRY WE'RE SO LATE! WE WERE ROBBING A PARTY STORE—

BROOKE'S MOM MADE US GET ALL THIS STUFF! SHE TOTES PAID.

...ZEKE!

YOU MADE IT, YAY!!

...

BROOKE, MANDY, SHAWNA—

THIS IS ZEKE! HE'S FROM THE YEARBOOK CLUB. I TOLD YOU ABOUT HIM.

Hiiiiiii♥!

YOU'RE WRITING AN ARTICLE ABOUT US!

UH... YEAH...

HI...

YOU HAVE *QUESTIONS.*

WE HAVE *ANSWERS.* ALL OF THEM.

...OH YEAH?

...

I GUESS HE'S NOT LEAVING ANYMORE?

...

NOPE.

....!

...IS SHE OKAY?

THERE YOU GUYS ARE!!

J AND J!

TWO OF MY FAVORITE PEOPLE!

LIIIIV! ♥

HA HAHAHA

TOSS

YOU GUYS ARE SO LATE!

I KNOOOW!

...

HA HA HA

HEY, WATCH THIS!

NO, IT'S MY TURN NEXT!

GO, GO, GO!

...AND JUST LIKE THAT, GARRETT'S PARTY WAS RAISED FROM THE DEAD.

BECAUSE LIV.

OOOOH, CAKE!

EVEN JAMES FINALLY SHOWED UP...

'SUP.

JAMES!

IT'S JAMES!

...

HI, JAMES!!!

...AND HAD FUN.

OMG, JAMES!!

WATCH OUT!!

GOOD SHOT!

GET IT, GET IT ...

GREAT PARTY, MAN!

SLAP

WHAT OTHER GAMES YOU GOT? DO YOU HAVE MADDEN?

...AND I GUESS ZEKE IS GETTING THE INTERVIEWS HE WANTED?

REALLY?

OH, YEAH. WE CAN SET UP A SPECIAL PHOTO SHOOT FOR YOU GUYS. WHATEVER YOU WANT.

FIDGET
FIDGET

H-HEY, GUYS!

JAZMINE, HEEEY!

I HAVE TO STEAL MY BOYFRIEND FOR A MINUTE, 'KAY?

...WHAT?

WHAT YOU DO MEAN, "WHAT"? WE WERE GOING TO LEAVE FIFTEEN MINUTES AGO!

OH, THAT! I ALREADY TEXTED MY PARENTS THAT I'M GONNA STAY LATER.

WHAT?!

WHEN WERE YOU GONNA TELL ME?!

YOU KNOW I HAVE AN EARLY CURFEW!

WELL, WELL THEN...

...THEN **GO HOME!**

NO ONE'S KEEPING YOU HERE, GEEZ!

RECOIL

...

WHAT IS THE PROBLEM HERE, **GOD!**

YOU WANNA GO, **GO.**

...

...OKAY.

I'LL GO.

ENJOY THE PARTY.

...

GOOD-BYE, ZEKE.

YEAH, YEAH. LATER!

# CHAPTER 5

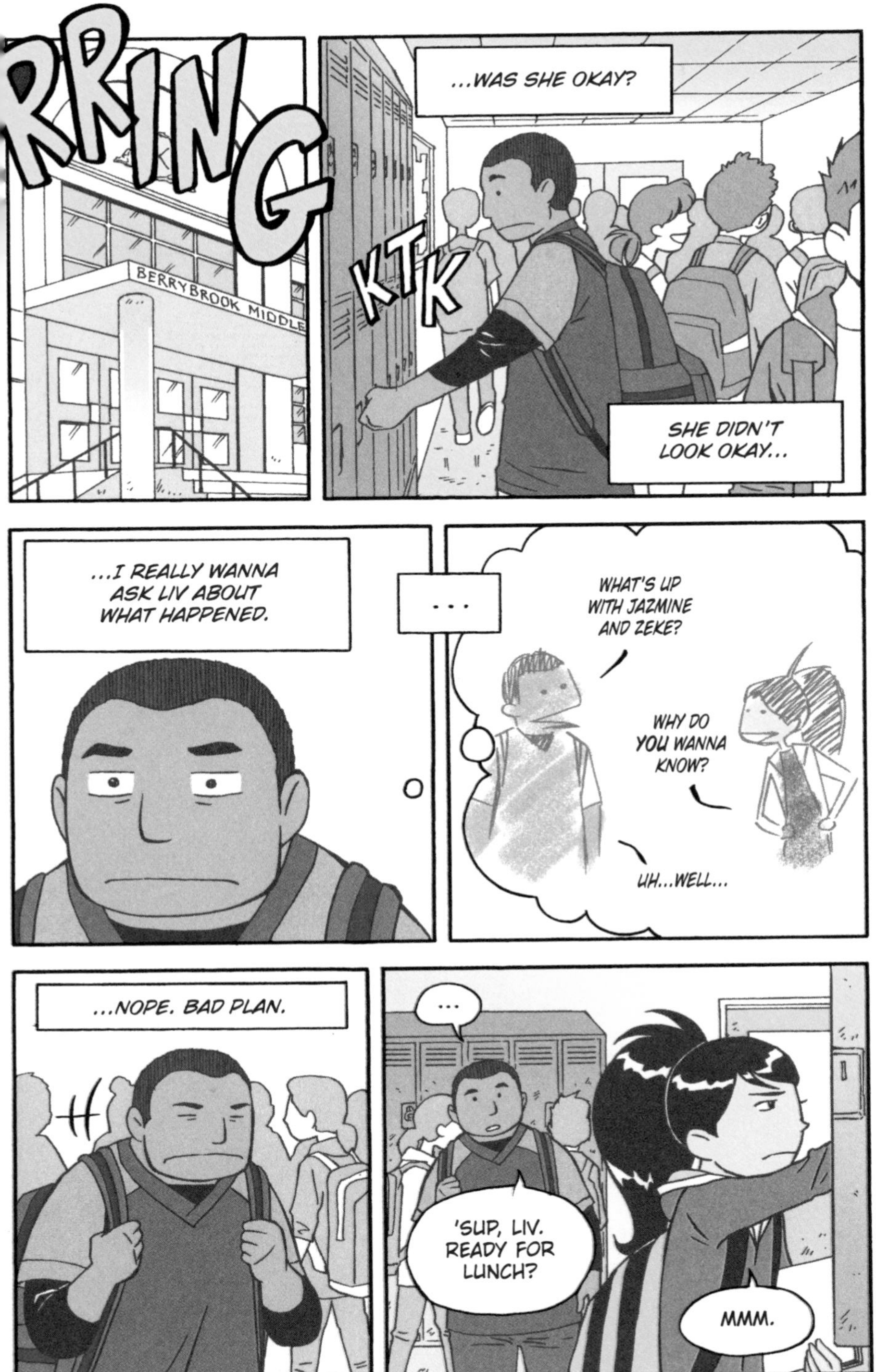
RRING
BERRYBROOK MIDDLE
...WAS SHE OKAY?
KTK
SHE DIDN'T LOOK OKAY...
...I REALLY WANNA ASK LIV ABOUT WHAT HAPPENED.
...
WHAT'S UP WITH JAZMINE AND ZEKE?
WHY DO YOU WANNA KNOW?
UH...WELL...
...NOPE. BAD PLAN.
...
'SUP, LIV. READY FOR LUNCH?
MMM.

...! YOU OKAY?

...YEAH.

I JUST GOT INTO THIS WEIRD TEXT-FIGHT WITH MARCUS YESTERDAY.

LIKE, WHAT DO *YOU* THINK?

IF YOU HAD A GIRLFRIEND, WOULD YOU DITCH HER AT A PARTY?

OR IF SHE DITCHED YOU FOR OTHER PEOPLE...

...WOULD YOU THINK IT'S TOTALLY OKAY AND NORMAL?

... N-NO?

WH-WHY ARE YOU ASK—

WELL, MARCUS WAS ALL, "WELL, HOW *CUTE* ARE THE OTHER GIRLS?" AND I WAS LIKE, "THAT'S NOT FUNNY," UGH!

*I MEAN, LOYALTY! LOOK IT UP!*

AND *GET* YOU SOME!

JORGE! OLIVIA!

HAVE YOU SEEN JAZMINE?

OH.

HELLO, ZEKE.

WHY'RE YOU LOOKING FOR HER, ZEKE?

....!

UH...

SHE...SHE SENT ME A WEIRD TEXT?

AND THEN STOPPED REPLYING.

SO I NEED TO FIND HER AND TALK—

"WEIRD TEXT"?

YOU MEAN THE ONE WHERE SHE BROKE UP WITH YOU?

...

....!

H-HOW DO YOU KNOW ABOUT THAT?!!

SHE'S MY FRIEND, ZEKE. SHE TELLS ME WHEN SHE BREAKS UP WITH A SLEAZEBALL!

H-HUH?

WHY DON'T YOU GO TALK TO THE GIRLS YOU DITCHED HER FOR YESTERDAY?

I-I...

I WAS JUST DOING RESEARCH! FOR THE ARTICLE!

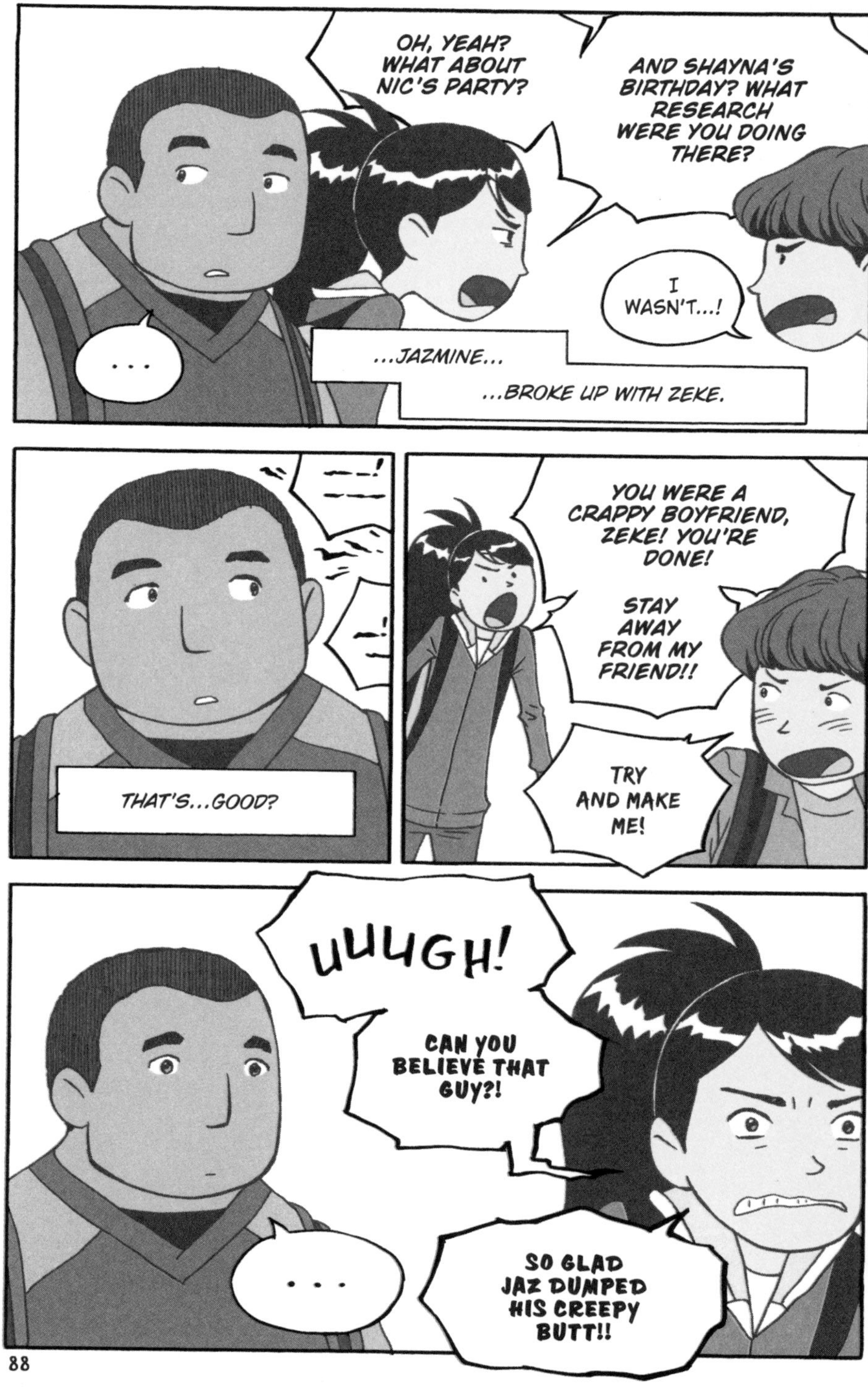
OH, YEAH? WHAT ABOUT NIC'S PARTY?
AND SHAYNA'S BIRTHDAY? WHAT RESEARCH WERE YOU DOING THERE?
I WASN'T...!
...
...JAZMINE...
...BROKE UP WITH ZEKE.
---!
--!
THAT'S...GOOD?
YOU WERE A CRAPPY BOYFRIEND, ZEKE! YOU'RE DONE!
STAY AWAY FROM MY FRIEND!!
TRY AND MAKE ME!
UUUGH!
CAN YOU BELIEVE THAT GUY?!
...
SO GLAD JAZ DUMPED HIS CREEPY BUTT!!

LUNCH.

...SHE BROKE UP WITH HIM?

OH, GOOD RIDDANCE!

I KNOW, RIGHT?

HE'S SUCH A TWO-FACE.

SHE SHOULD DATE SOMEONE WHO'S, LIKE, *NOT* A JERK!

...

OOOOH, I KNOW! LET'S SET HER UP!

...

YEAH!!

WITH SOMEONE *NICE!*

WHO WON'T DITCH HER AT A PARTY!

YEAH, YEAH! SOMEONE *RELIABLE!*

AND *LOYAL!*

G U L P

WHO DO WE KNOW LIKE THAT?

OOH!

*ALEX!*

...

TCH

ALEX... BASKETBALL ALEX?

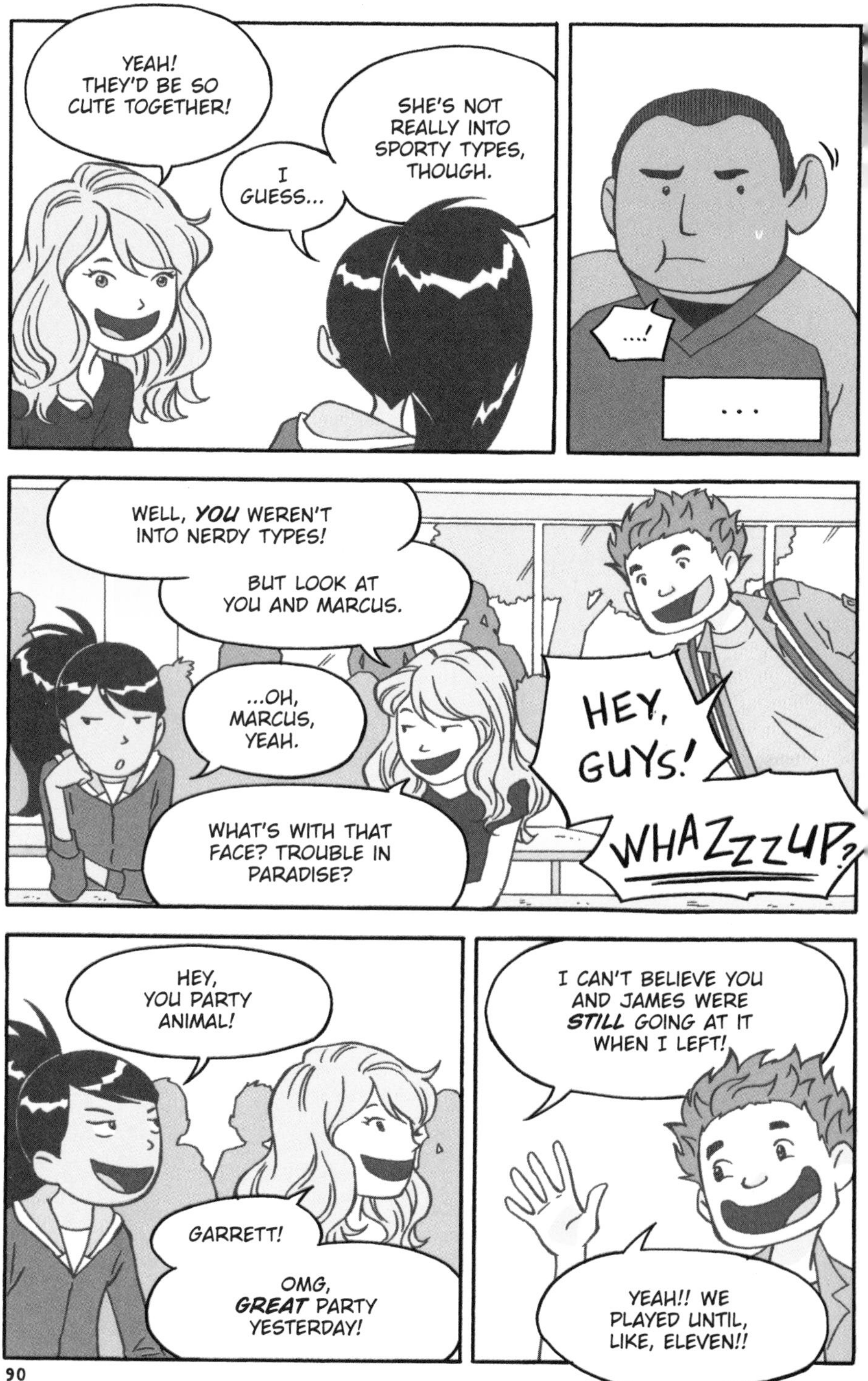
YEAH! THEY'D BE SO CUTE TOGETHER!
I GUESS...
SHE'S NOT REALLY INTO SPORTY TYPES, THOUGH.
...!
. . .
WELL, YOU WEREN'T INTO NERDY TYPES!
BUT LOOK AT YOU AND MARCUS.
...OH, MARCUS, YEAH.
WHAT'S WITH THAT FACE? TROUBLE IN PARADISE?
HEY, GUYS!
WHAZZZUP?!
HEY, YOU PARTY ANIMAL!
GARRETT!
OMG, GREAT PARTY YESTERDAY!
I CAN'T BELIEVE YOU AND JAMES WERE STILL GOING AT IT WHEN I LEFT!
YEAH!! WE PLAYED UNTIL, LIKE, ELEVEN!!

JAMES TOTALLY WON...

...BUT WE'RE GONNA HAVE A REMATCH AT HIS PLACE THIS WEEKEND!

JORGE, HE SAID YOU SHOULD COME TOO!

...

UH.

NAW, I'M GOOD.

...GARRETT'S SO EXCITED...

COULD IT BE HIS... NEW BROMANCE?

SH-SHUT UP!

...BUT, YES.

...WELL, ANYWAY, BACK TO JAZMINE.

RIGHT!

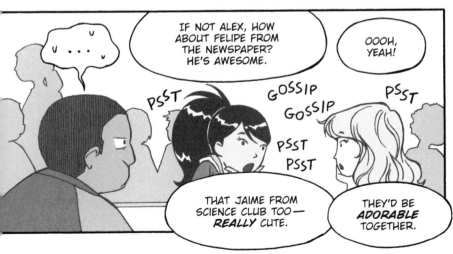

....

IF NOT ALEX, HOW ABOUT FELIPE FROM THE NEWSPAPER? HE'S AWESOME.

OOOH, YEAH!

PSST

GOSSIP GOSSIP

PSST

PSST PSST

PSST

THAT JAIME FROM SCIENCE CLUB TOO— *REALLY* CUTE.

THEY'D BE *ADORABLE* TOGETHER.

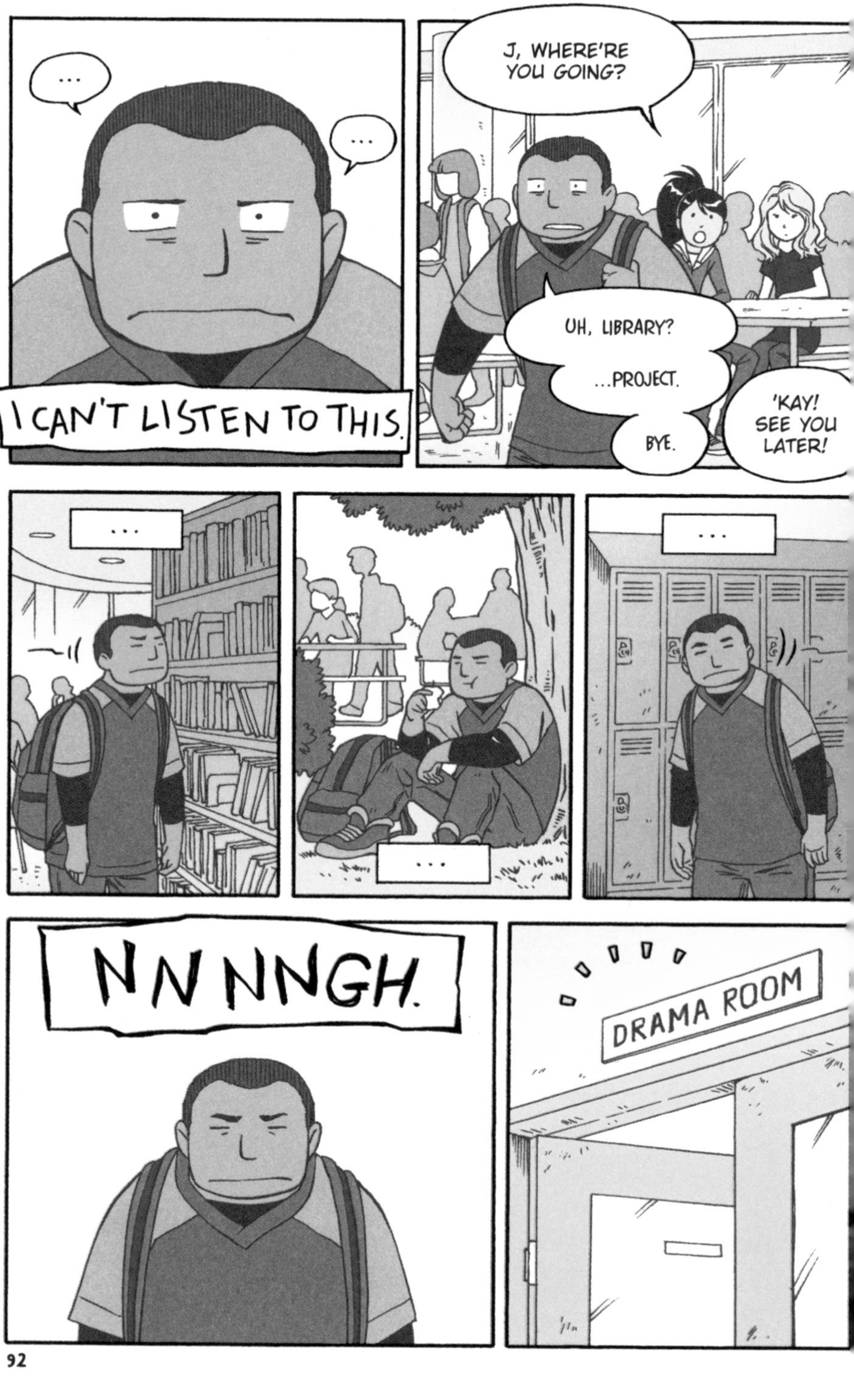
...
...
I CAN'T LISTEN TO THIS.
J, WHERE'RE YOU GOING?
UH, LIBRARY?
...PROJECT.
BYE.
'KAY! SEE YOU LATER!
...
...
...
NNNNGH.
DRAMA ROOM

...SHE'S PROBABLY NOT EVEN HERE.

I KNOW SHE'S HERE!

LET ME IN!

JAZMINE!

PUSH

I JUST WANNA TALK!

UGH, GO AWAY!

PUSH

PUSH

SHE DOESN'T WANT TO SEE YOU!

...THIS GUY.

JAZMINE!!

YOU CAN'T JUST BLOCK ME!

GO AWAY!!

SHOO!

IS THERE A PROBLEM HERE?

....!

Y-YEAH! THERE IS!

I WANNA TALK TO JAZMINE, BUT THEY WON'T LET ME IN—

...

...DOES SHE WANNA TALK TO YOU?

...HUH...?

NO, SHE DOESN'T!!

SHE'S DONE TALKING TO YOU!

SHE HAS TO LET ME EXPLAIN—

WEDGE

LOOOM

DUDE, NO.

SHE *REALLY* DOESN'T.

SO LEAVE IT ALONE.

WH-WHA...?

I JUST...

...WANT TO EXPLAIN—

AND IT SOUNDS LIKE SHE DOESN'T WANT TO LISTEN.

RESPECT THAT.

NO WAY! SHE'S *GOTTA* GIVE ME A CHANCE TO—

THIS. GUY!!

BUDDY, ARE YOU THICK?

SHE. DOESN'T. OWE. YOU. ANYTHING.

YOU'RE STALKING AND HARASSING.

*GET LOST.*

THAT'S RIGHT, YOU'RE A TOTAL STALKER!!

GO AWAY BEFORE I CALL MRS. FERRIS!

....!

Y-YOU ALL *SUCK!*

UGH, WHY'S HE SUCH A CREEP ALL OF A SUDDEN?!

HE SEEMED SO NICE...

THANKS FOR CHASING HIM OFF, SHERIFF!

LATER!

KTK

....!

...

...I GUESS I SHOULDN'T STICK AROUND...

...OR I'LL LOOK LIKE A STALKER TOO...

THESE THINGS ALWAYS LOOK SO MUCH EASIER IN MOVIES.

UGH.

JORGE! YOU PROTECTED ME!

LET'S GO TO THE ATHLETICS BALL TOGETHER!

I GUESS THAT'S WHY YOU CAN PREDICT MOVIE PLOTS...

SEE YA!

BYE!

DON'T WE HAVE CLUB TODAY?

...BUT CAN'T PREDICT LIFE.

...!

HAHA

GOSSIP GOSSIP

...THEY'RE JUST GONNA GOSSIP ABOUT DATES FOR JAZMINE.

SO NOT HERE FOR THIS.

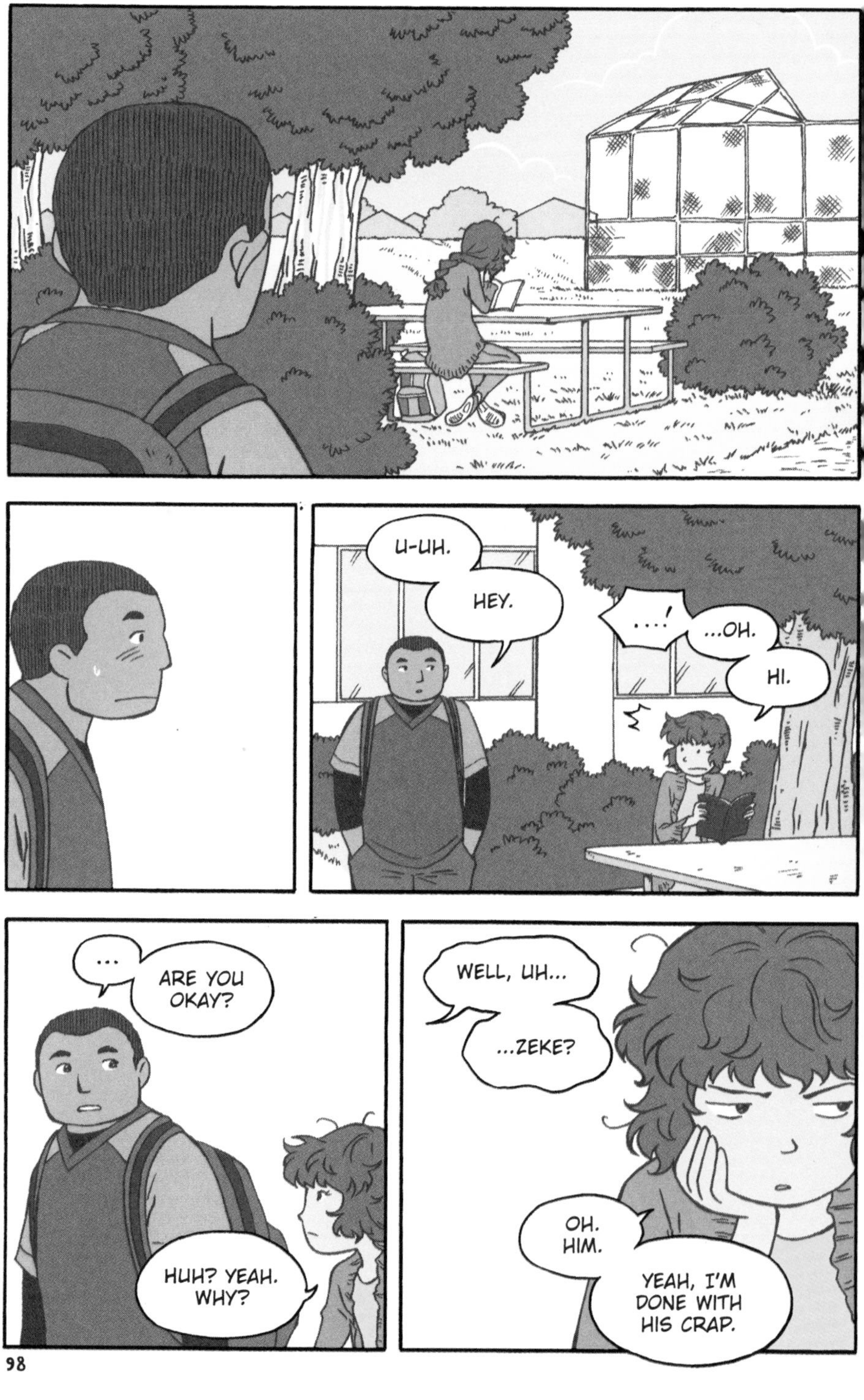
U-UH.
HEY.
...!
...OH.
HI.
...
ARE YOU OKAY?
HUH? YEAH. WHY?
WELL, UH...
...ZEKE?
OH. HIM.
YEAH, I'M DONE WITH HIS CRAP.

...

...

...OH, DID YOU SEE OLIVIA AND BROOKE?

HAVE THEY LEFT YET?

OH, UH...

I THINK SO?

OH, *GOOD.*

I CAN STOP HIDING.

I MEAN, I KNOW THEY MEAN WELL, BUT *UGH.*

THEY WERE SO ANNOYING TODAY.

IT'S LIKE THEY'RE TRYING TO ARRANGE MY MARRIAGE.

...OH!

I HEARD ZEKE WAS HARASSING NIC AND EVERYONE TODAY...

...BUT YOU HELPED CHASE HIM OFF?

UH...

YEAH.

THANK YOU.

YOU'RE A REALLY GOOD PERSON, JORGE.

...

WELL, I'LL SEE YOU AROUND!

...NO.

WAIT.

...

...I HAVE TO SAY SOMETHING.

ANYTHING.

UH.

W-WAIT!

HM?

W-WOULD YOU EVER...

...G-GO TO THE ATHLETICS BALL? W-WITH ME?

....!

... ...

... AH...

ATHLETICS BALL...?

Y-YEAH.

WITH YOU...?

UH, LIKE...

...LIKE A DATE?

...

...

Y-YEAH...?

OH.

um...

...

...

...OKAY.

...OKAY?

...Y-YEAH.

...OKAY.

OKAY.

COOL.

WHAAAAAT.

# CHAPTER 6

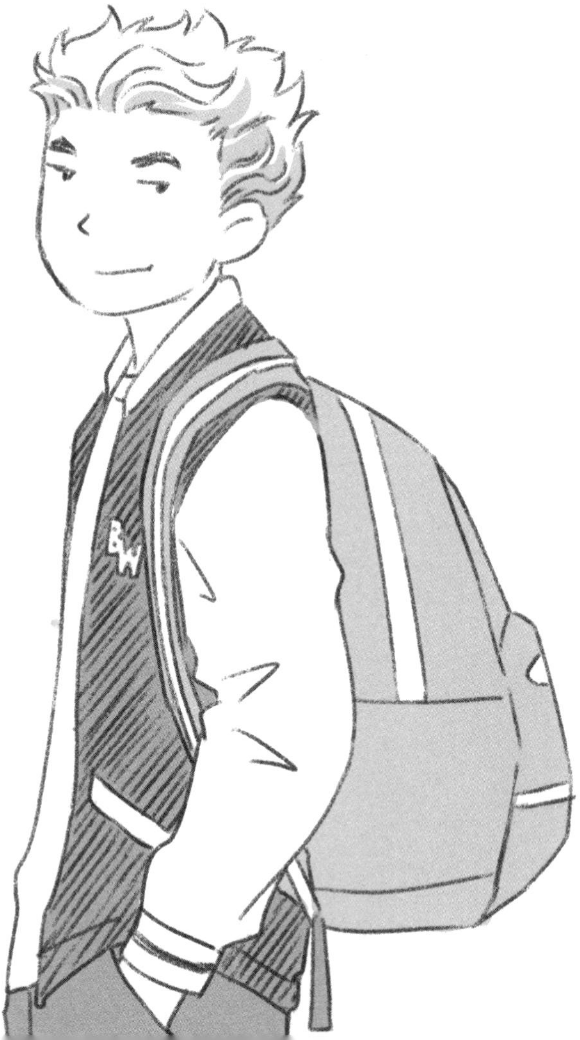
BW

NEXT DAY.

ATHLETICS BALL...? WITH ME?

OKAY.

DID THAT...

DID THAT REALLY HAPPEN?

I JUST BLURTED THAT OUT.

K
T
K

DIDN'T KNOW SHE'D SAY *YES!*

...I HAVE NO IDEA WHAT TO DO NOW.

JORGE, HEY!

MORNING!

'SUP, SHERIFF.

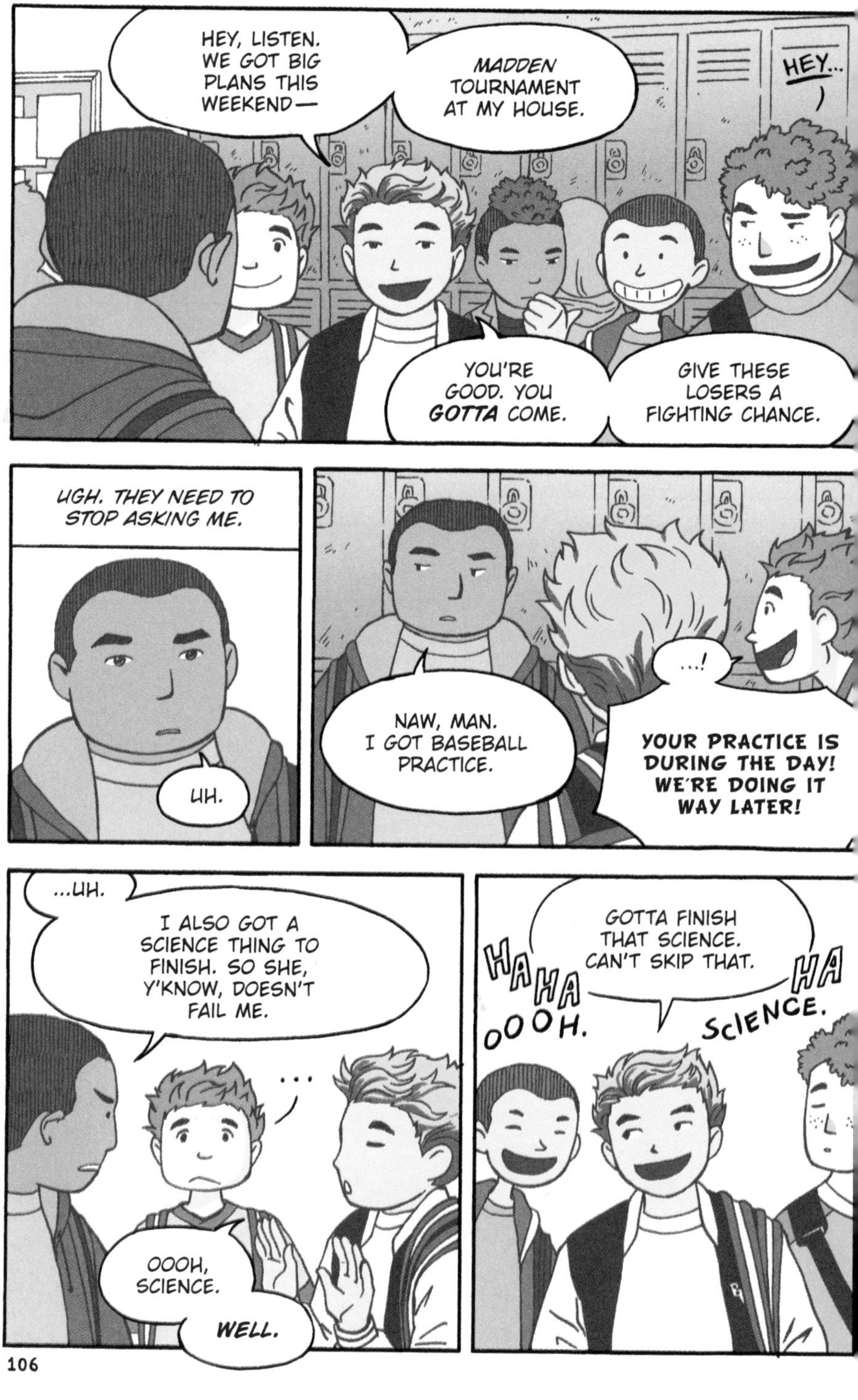
HEY, LISTEN. WE GOT BIG PLANS THIS WEEKEND—
*MADDEN* TOURNAMENT AT MY HOUSE.
HEY...
YOU'RE GOOD. YOU **GOTTA** COME.
GIVE THESE LOSERS A FIGHTING CHANCE.
*UGH. THEY NEED TO STOP ASKING ME.*
UH.
NAW, MAN. I GOT BASEBALL PRACTICE.
...!
**YOUR PRACTICE IS DURING THE DAY! WE'RE DOING IT WAY LATER!**
...UH.
I ALSO GOT A SCIENCE THING TO FINISH. SO SHE, Y'KNOW, DOESN'T FAIL ME.
...
OOOH, SCIENCE.
**WELL.**
HA HA HA
OOOH.
GOTTA FINISH THAT SCIENCE. CAN'T SKIP THAT.
HA
SCIENCE.

WELL, SEE YOU LATER, EGGHEAD.

HA HA

...

...C'MON, YOU COULD TOTALLY TRY TO MAKE IT!

WHAT *GIVES*?

...

HEY, UH...

DON'T TRY TO SET ME UP WITH THOSE GUYS, 'KAY?

THEY'RE TOTAL TROLLS WHEN THEY PLAY.

*NOT* MY THING.

WHAAA—?

YOU MEAN THE WAY THEY TALK? IT'S JUST FOR LAUGHS. THEY DON'T *MEAN* ANY OF THAT!

YEAH, RIGHT...

LOOK—

YOU WANNA HANG WITH THEM, FINE. IT'S A FREE COUNTRY.

BUT I'M NOT GONNA.

SORRY, MAN.

...HOPE THAT WAS THE END OF *THAT.*

...RIGHT.

OF COURSE SHE'D KNOW — SHE AND JAZMINE TALK ALL THE TIME.

UH...

UM...

YOU KNOW...

I DON'T!!

I DIDN'T EVEN KNOW YOU LIKED HER!!

WHY DIDN'T YOU TELL ME?!

THIS IS SO AMAZING!!

TWO OF MY FAVORITE BUDDIES!! DATING!!

I'M SO HAPPY!!

SHH! K-KEEP IT DOWN!

I CAN'T!! AAAAAA♥

...WAAAIT.

IS THIS WHY YOU'VE BEEN SO WEIRD LATELY?

...

OMG, I KNEW IT! I KNEW SOMETHING WAS UP!

HA HA

YOU WERE CRUSHING ON JAZMINE!!

OF COURSE!

UH, I-I HAVE TO GO.

...!

....!

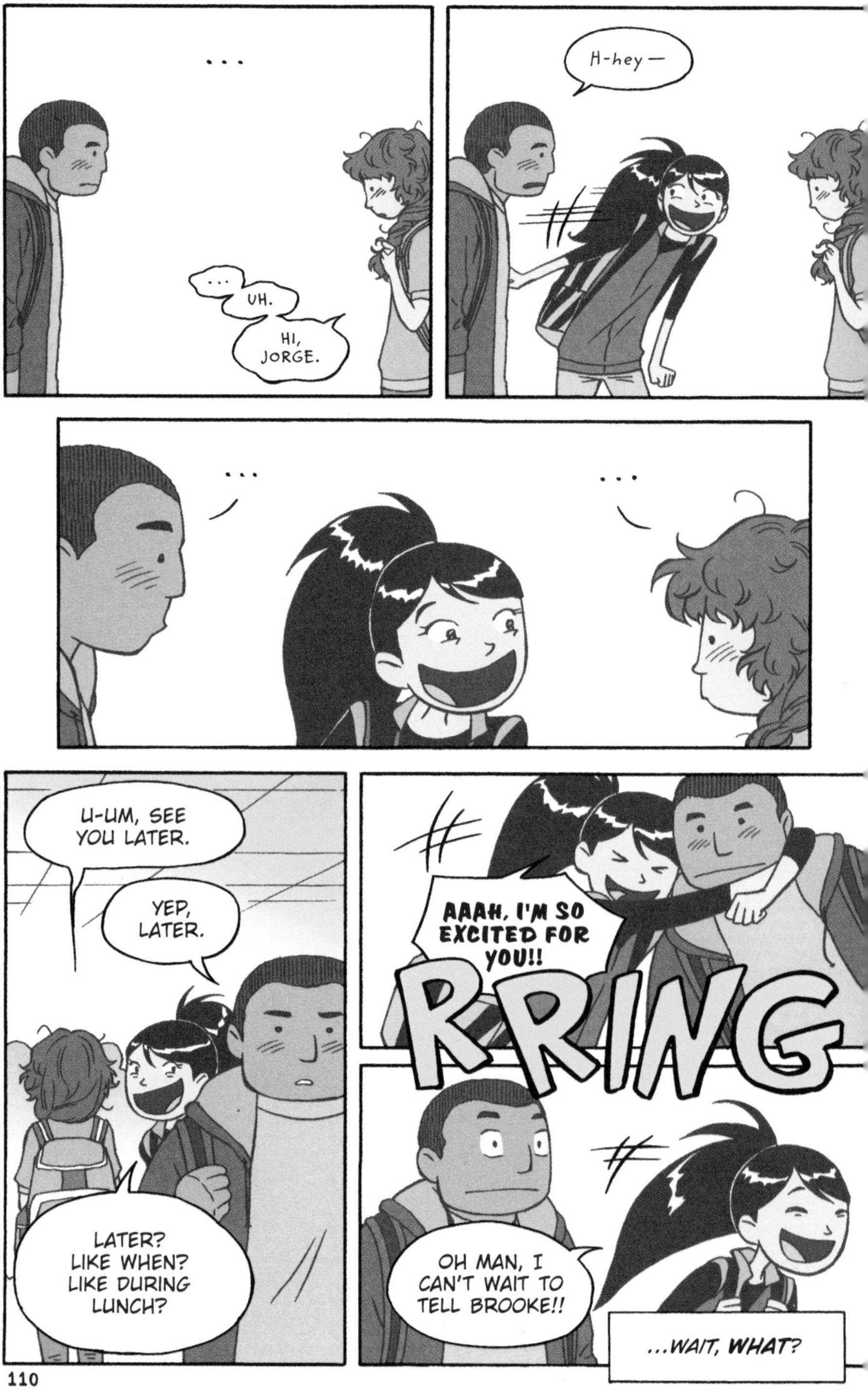
...
...
UH.
HI, JORGE.
H-hey—
...
...
U-UM, SEE YOU LATER.
YEP, LATER.
LATER? LIKE WHEN? LIKE DURING LUNCH?
AAAH, I'M SO EXCITED FOR YOU!!
RRING
OH MAN, I CAN'T WAIT TO TELL BROOKE!!
...WAIT, WHAT?

...I FORGOT. THIS WHOLE SCHOOL IS A GIANT GOSSIP MACHINE.

LUNCH IS GONNA *SUCK*.

HI, JORGE.

...

...I WONDER IF SHE'D WANT TO EAT LUNCH TOGETHER.

RRRING

...I SHOULD ASK...

...BUT SHE'S NOT IN ANY OF MY CLUBS OR CLASSES.

....!

...DUH.

I SHOULD ASK FOR HER PHONE NUMBER!

111

LUNCH.

DRAMA ROO[M]

WELL, *HELLO*.

WHO HAVE WE HERE?

IS IT JORGE?!

I WANNA SEE.

UUUGH.

YOUR PRINCESS IS NOT IN THIS CASTLE.

I THINK SHE'S IN THE LIBR—

OKAY, BYE.

*BOY,* GOSSIP WORKS FAST.

LIBRARY

LOOK

LOOK

...SHE'S NOT HERE EITHER.

...

...OLIVIA HAS HER NUMBER.

♡ ♡ ♡ H...

WANT HER NUUUMBER? OOH-LA-LA!

...

...WORTH IT. GONNA ASK.

HEY, LIV!

OH.

HEY.

!

...

SIT

...

DUDE, UH...

YOU ALL RIGHT?

...

DO YOU THINK I'M *NEEDY*?

.....!!

...WHAT? *NO*.

...SOMEONE SAY THAT TO YOU?

...*MARCUS.*

WHAT THE...?

YOU'RE, LIKE, KICK-ASS INDEPENDENT.

WHAT'S HIS PROBLEM?

...WELL...

YOU KNOW HOW WE GOT THE ATHLETICS BALL? IT'S A BIG DEAL?

YEAH?

WELL, *HE* KNOWS TOO, AND I KINDA ASSUMED THAT...THAT HE'D COME? WITH ME?

BUT...

...HE SAID THAT'S JUST ME BEING *NEEDY.*

THAT HE'S GOT SOME BIG ONLINE GAME LAUNCH TO WATCH THAT NIGHT.

....!

I MEAN, I WENT TO THAT BOARD GAME THING WITH HIM.

GUH, IT WAS SO BORING...

...BUT, LIKE, IT'S WHAT YOU DO, RIGHT?

YOU SUPPORT EACH OTHER'S... STUFF...!

...

WHY WON'T HE SUPPORT MINE?

...

...I'M LESS IMPORTANT THAN A *GAME* TO HIM.

...

...SUDDEN URGE...

...TO DESTROY MARCUS.

**THUD**

HEY, GUYS!

THE THUNDERNATOR HAS ARRIVED!

...THE **WHAT**?

IT'S MY NEW PLAYER TAG! MADE IT LAST NIGHT, FOR JAMES'S CREW!

COOL, HUH?

HUH.

WAIT, SO YOU **WERE** ONLINE YESTERDAY?

YEAH! JAMES SENT ME AN INVITE OUT OF THE BLUE!

WE PLAYED, LIKE, THREE MISSIONS!

WHAT?? I KEPT PINGING YOU, BUT YOU NEVER REPLIED!

...OH YEAH, I SAW THOSE, LIKE, WAAAY LATER!

MY CHAT WAS **BLOWING UP**! I THINK JAMES'S WHOLE CREW WAS THERE.

IT WAS **AMAZING**!

EVER SINCE THE PARTY, I'M FINALLY ONE OF THE GUYS!

...

BOY, I'M SURE GLAD I SET *THAT* UP FOR YOU.

WITH NO *THANKS* OR ANYTHING.

...OH YEAH!

THANKS!

YOU'RE THE BEST!

PFFT, WHATEVER.

WE'RE STILL ON TO PLAY TONIGHT, RIGHT?

I NEED SOME MINDLESS FPS ACTION.

NO CAN DO!

THUNDERNATOR IS IN HIGH DEMAND TONIGHT—JAMES IS PLANNING A—

UUGH, NEVER MIND!!

JORGE, WILL YOU PLAY WITH ME?

SURE.

HOMEWORK FIRST, THOUGH.

...HOMEWORK!!

CRAP.

WE PLAYED SO LATE LAST NIGHT...

...I FORGOT TO DO MY MATH HOMEWORK!

LIV, CAN I COPY YOURS AGAIN?

LAST TIME, I *PROMISE.*

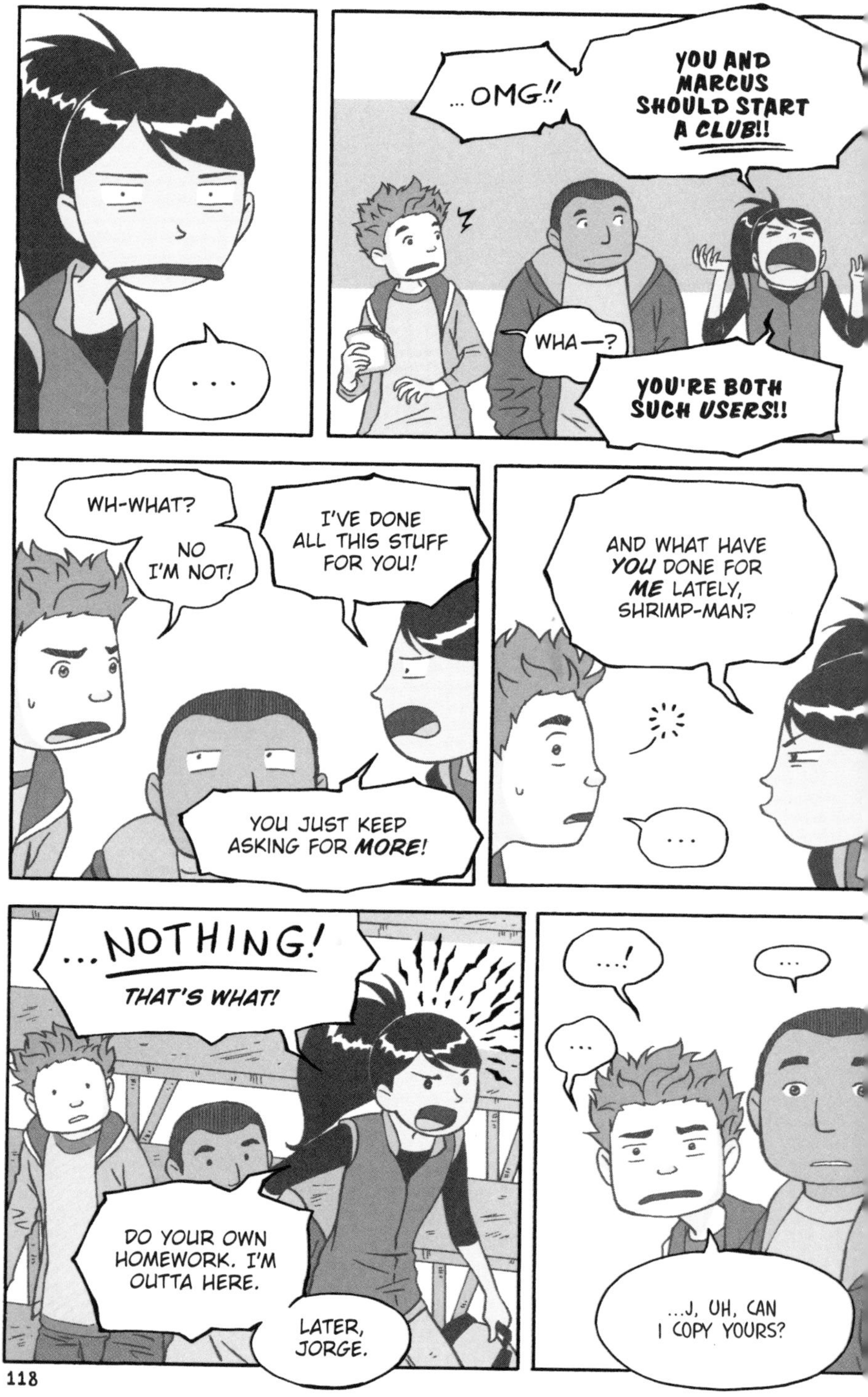
...
...OMG!!
YOU AND MARCUS SHOULD START A CLUB!!
WHA—?
YOU'RE BOTH SUCH USERS!!
WH-WHAT?
NO I'M NOT!
I'VE DONE ALL THIS STUFF FOR YOU!
YOU JUST KEEP ASKING FOR MORE!
AND WHAT HAVE YOU DONE FOR ME LATELY, SHRIMP-MAN?
...
...NOTHING!
THAT'S WHAT!
DO YOUR OWN HOMEWORK. I'M OUTTA HERE.
LATER, JORGE.
...!
...
...
...J, UH, CAN I COPY YOURS?

...WELL, SO MUCH FOR GETTING JAZMINE'S NUMBER FROM LIV...

SEE YOU!

IS THE BUS HERE?

DRAMA ROOM

HA HA HA

...

...SHE'S PROBABLY NOT HERE AGAIN.

FWEET

YAMMER

CHATTER

HA HA

SETTLE DOWN, EVERYONE! ATHLETICS CLUB IS NOW IN SESSION!

GOOD NEWS—

THE ATHLETICS BALL TICKETS ARE OFFICIALLY SOLD OUT!

YEEEAH!! WOO! ~YAY!

TIME TO GET SERIOUS ABOUT THE ORGANIZING COMMITTEE.

WE NEED VOLUNTEERS FOR—

HEY, LIV.

YOU OKAY?

Nnrgh.

...WANT ME TO DESTROY MARCUS?

...WHAT? HA-HA, NO.

...THANKS, THOUGH.

YOU SURE? I COULD INTRODUCE HIM TO MY TWO FRIENDS—

YOU DORK.

"GOOD"...

...AND "MANNERS."

HA HA HA

OLIVIA.

BROOKE.

CAN I COUNT ON YOU TWO AS LIAISONS TO THE ART AND DRAMA CLUBS?

WE COULD USE THEIR HELP WITH THE DECORATIONS AND PROPS.

....!

ABSOLUTELY, MRS. RASHAD. WE'RE ON IT.

AND JORGE WANTS TO VOLUNTEER TOO!

ESPECIALLY TO HELP LIAISON WITH THE DRAMA CLUB.

....!

GREAT! PUTTING YOU THREE DOWN FOR THAT. NEXT—

You're welcome, buddy.

...LIV'S A REALLY, **REALLY** GOOD FRIEND.

DRAMA ROOM

KNOCK, KNOCK! ANYONE HOME? THE ATHLETICS L'AISONNNS ARE HERE!!

...LIV!

SOOO, WE NEED YOU GUYS' HELP WITH OUR BALL.

WHICH BALL? SOCCER BALL? OR FOOTBA—

THAT IS THE WORST JOKE, NIC.

GLANCE

LOOK

IS THAT YOUR NEW BOYFRIEND?

SH-SHUT UUUP!

...

JAZMINE, THERE YOU ARE!

...

WE NEED YOUR HEEEELP!

...

...I CAN DO THIS.

"CAN I GET YOUR NUMBER?"

EXCEPT OUT LOUD.

...JAZMINE KNOWS WHERE ALL OF THE STUFF IS!

JAZ, WHERE ARE ALL THE "STARDUST" PROP BOXES?

OH, THOSE, YEAH!

WE'D HAVE TO DIG THEM OUT OF MRS. F'S OFFICE.

THIS ONE?

YEAH, AND THE ONE BELOW!

JORGE, COULD YOU GRAB THAT BAG TOO?

...

...I LIKE HEARING HER SAY MY NAME...

GLANCE

. . .

. . .

N-NOW OR NEVER.

. . .

Um.

C-can I get your number?

To, like, text...?

. . . . !

. . .

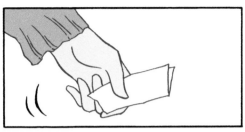

RUSTLE
RUMMAGE

?

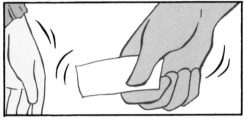

...Wh- what's this?

...

...My number.

I was gonna slide it in your locker today.

!

Hide it before the gossip-hounds see.

HA HA

....!

# CHAPTER 7

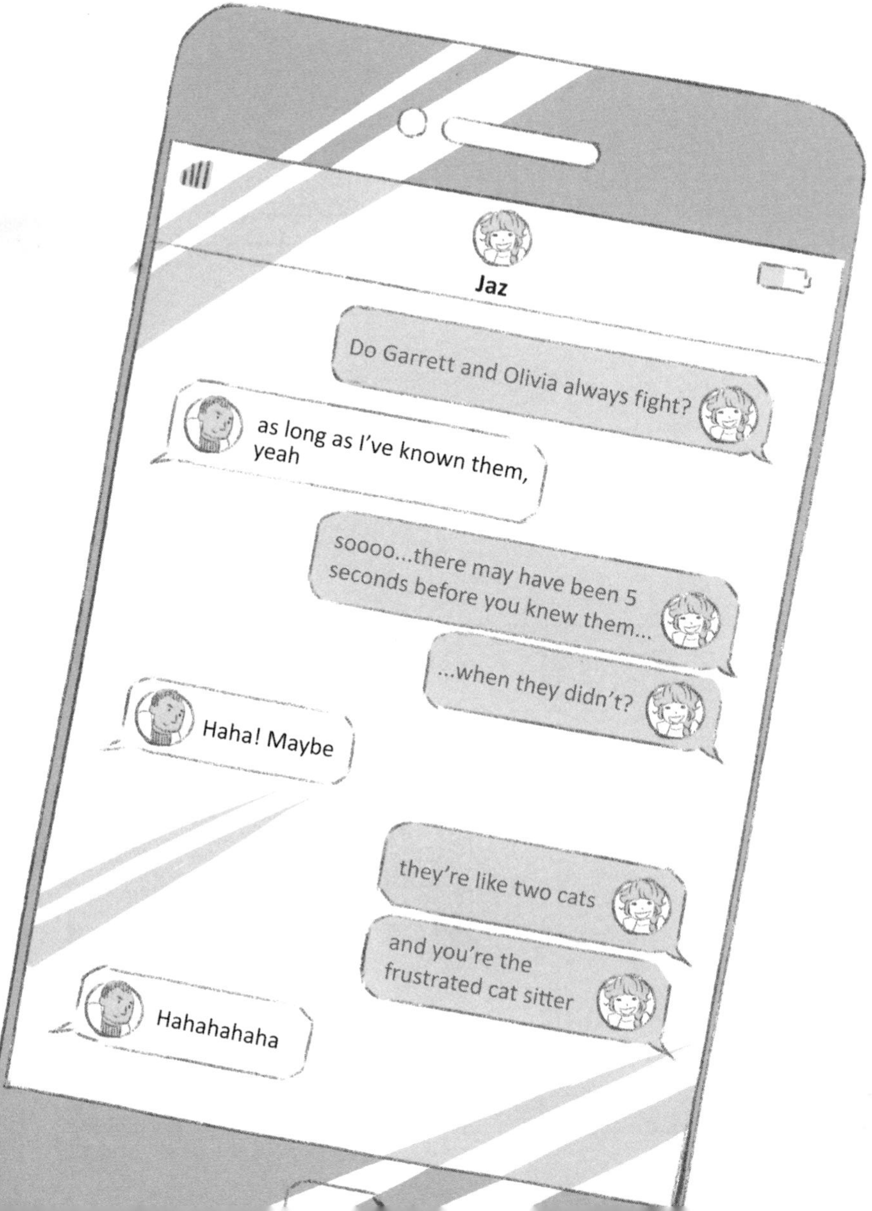
Jaz
Do Garrett and Olivia always fight?
as long as I've known them, yeah
soooo...there may have been 5 seconds before you knew them...
...when they didn't?
Haha! Maybe
they're like two cats
and you're the frustrated cat sitter
Hahahahaha

A MONDAY.

'EY, JORGE!!

DID YOU GUYS REALLY WIN WITH A 10TH INNING YESTERDAY?

YEP.

YO, CONGRATS!

ARE YOU PLAYING FOXDALE NEXT?

NO. RIVERSIDE, I THINK.

KICK THEIR BUTTS!

LATER!

HA-HA, 'KAY.

JORGE!! DO YOU HAVE THE SCIENCE PROJECT NOTES?!

I FORGOT MINE!

YEAH, I GOT 'EM.

YOU NEED?

YESSS!!

I'LL BORROW DURING LUNCH, OKAY?

SURE.

THANKS, MAN!!

SLAM

...IT'S BEEN BUSY LATELY.

SCHOOL, PRACTICE, ATHLETICS BALL PREP...

I HAD TWO BASEBALL GAMES.

...JAZMINE CAME TO THE LAST ONE.

RRING

CLASS DISMISSED! REMEMBER YOUR BOOK REPORTS NEXT WEEK!

WE TEXT EVERY DAY NOW.

I'M REAL BAD AT IT.

NEVER KNOW WHAT TO SAY.

SHE'S ACE AT IT, THOUGH.

SHE'LL TEXT ME THE **MOST RANDOM** STUFF. OR SOMETHING REALLY *FUNNY*.

(AND IT'LL USUALLY HAVE A HEDGEHOG STICKER. SHE'S GOT A REAL THING FOR THEM.)

I ALWAYS REPLY AS SOON AS I GET IT.

WHATEVER IT IS.

...I CAN'T WAIT FOR THE ATHLETICS BALL.

JORGE.

POP!

GUH!

ATHLETICS MEET INSTEAD OF LUNCH TODAY— DON'T FORGET!!

GRAB YOUR FOOD AND HEAD OVER TO THE GYM.

YEAH, YEAH.

COOL IT, BOSSY.

...OLIVIA'S STARTED DIALING ME INTO THEIR GROUP CHATS TOO.

JAZMINE, HEY!

SOME **REAL** AWKWARD ONES.

LIKE WHEN SHE FINALLY BROKE UP WITH MARCUS (GOOD RIDDANCE) —

THAT WAS THE NIGHT OF A THOUSAND TEXTS *I DIDN'T WANT.*

UGH.

OH, AND LAST BUT NOT LEAST...

JORGE, HEY!!

LUNCH?

...THERE'S THE GARRETT PROBLEM.

...WELL, THE GARRETT AND *JAMES* PROBLEM.

'SUP, JORGE.

...

*AWESOME* GAME THIS WEEKEND!

CONGRATS!

UH, THANKS.

YOU GOT LUNCH PLANS?

...JUST GONNA GRAB SOME FOOD QUICK AND HEAD OVER TO THE MEET.

OH YEAH?

US TOO!

WE'LL COME WITH YOU!

SLAP

....!

...CRAP.

NO REASON FOR ME TO SAY NO...

O-OKAY.

LET'S GRAB SOMETHING QUICK.

YAAAY!

ROLL OUT, YOU CLOWNS!

HEY, DID YOU SEE THAT VIDEO I SENT?

NOT YET. IT'S GOOD?

IT'S **SO** FUNNY.

...I SENT IT TO LIV TOO...

...BUT SHE DIDN'T REPLY.

I THINK SHE'S STILL MAD AT ME.

...

...SHE IS.

LIV WAS ALREADY ANGRY AT HIM FROM BEFORE... BUT THEN, WHEN SHE BROKE UP WITH MARCUS...

...THIS IDIOT DECIDED TO RUB SOME **SALT** ON THAT—

HA HA!

**TOLD** YA YOU WERE STUPID FOR DATING HIM!

YOU HAVE THE WORST TASTE IN BOYFRIENDS, MAN.

SO NOW THEY'RE NOT TALKING. (WELL, HE'S TALKING. LIV ISN'T.)

?

!

...

...

...AND I'M STUCK IN THE MIDDLE.

...AND IT DOESN'T HELP THAT HE'S HANGING OUT WITH JAMES MORE THAN WITH US...

...

...

AWW, **MAN.**

...WHY IS THE LINE SO LONG ALREADY?

THIS'LL TAKE FOREVER.

NAW.

I GOT A *TRICK.*

WATCH THE PRO WORK.

HEY, GORGEOUS.

HEY!

BUMP

WE'RE LATE FOR A CLUB MEETING...

...!

*SLIDE*

MIND IF WE CUT IN? ♥

UM.

....

...

G-GO AHEAD...?

WOO!

C'MON, GUYS!

....!

THIS KIND-HEARTED ANGEL IS LETTING US GO FIRST!

NO! *AGAIN?*

YEEAAH!

ALL RIGHT!

WAIT, WHAT?

HEY!

NO!

....!

JAMES!

DUDE, WHAT ARE YOU DOING?

....?

GETTING... FOOD?

THEY WERE HERE **FIRST**!

AND WE'RE **NOT** LATE! WE GOT TONS OF TIME!

...

...

...PFFT, FINE, WHATEVER.

WAS JUST TRYING TO HELP.

YOU WERE SO WORRIED ABOUT BEING **LATE**.

*WHAT...?!*

HE'S MAKING IT **MY** FAULT?

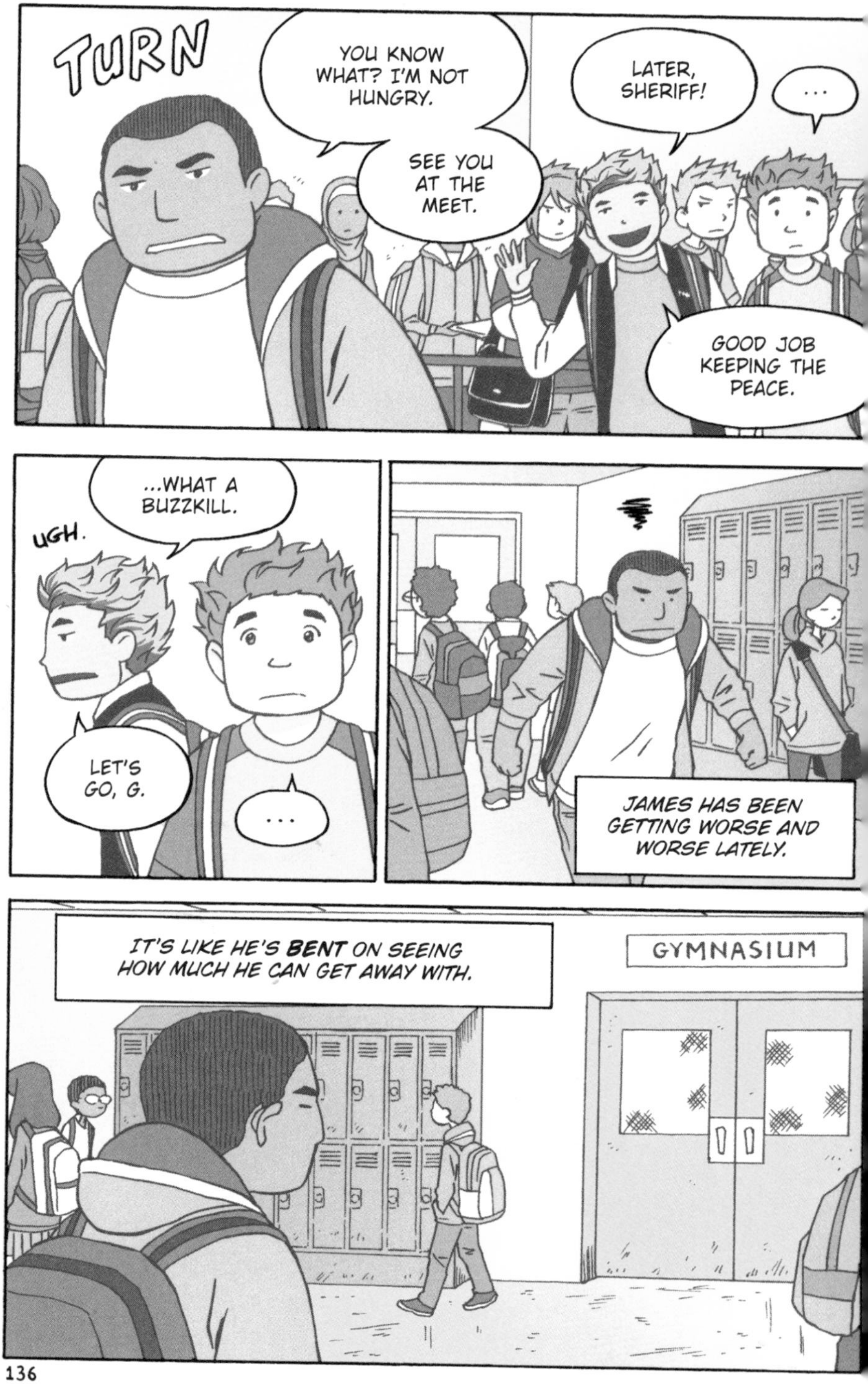
TURN
YOU KNOW WHAT? I'M NOT HUNGRY.
SEE YOU AT THE MEET.
LATER, SHERIFF!
...
GOOD JOB KEEPING THE PEACE.
...WHAT A BUZZKILL.
UGH.
LET'S GO, G.
...
JAMES HAS BEEN GETTING WORSE AND WORSE LATELY.
IT'S LIKE HE'S **BENT** ON SEEING HOW MUCH HE CAN GET AWAY WITH.
GYMNASIUM

...

...WHY DOES GARRETT HANG OUT WITH HIM...?

JORGE, HEY!

OVER HERE!

HEY, ACTION GUY.

SAVED YOU A SPOT!

HIIIII, JORGE! WE CAME TO HELP WITH THE PLANNING!

WHERE'S YOUR FOOD?

DID YOU ALREADY EAT?

UH, NO...

I FORGOT IT.

YOU FORGOT YOUR FOOD...?

OH NO!

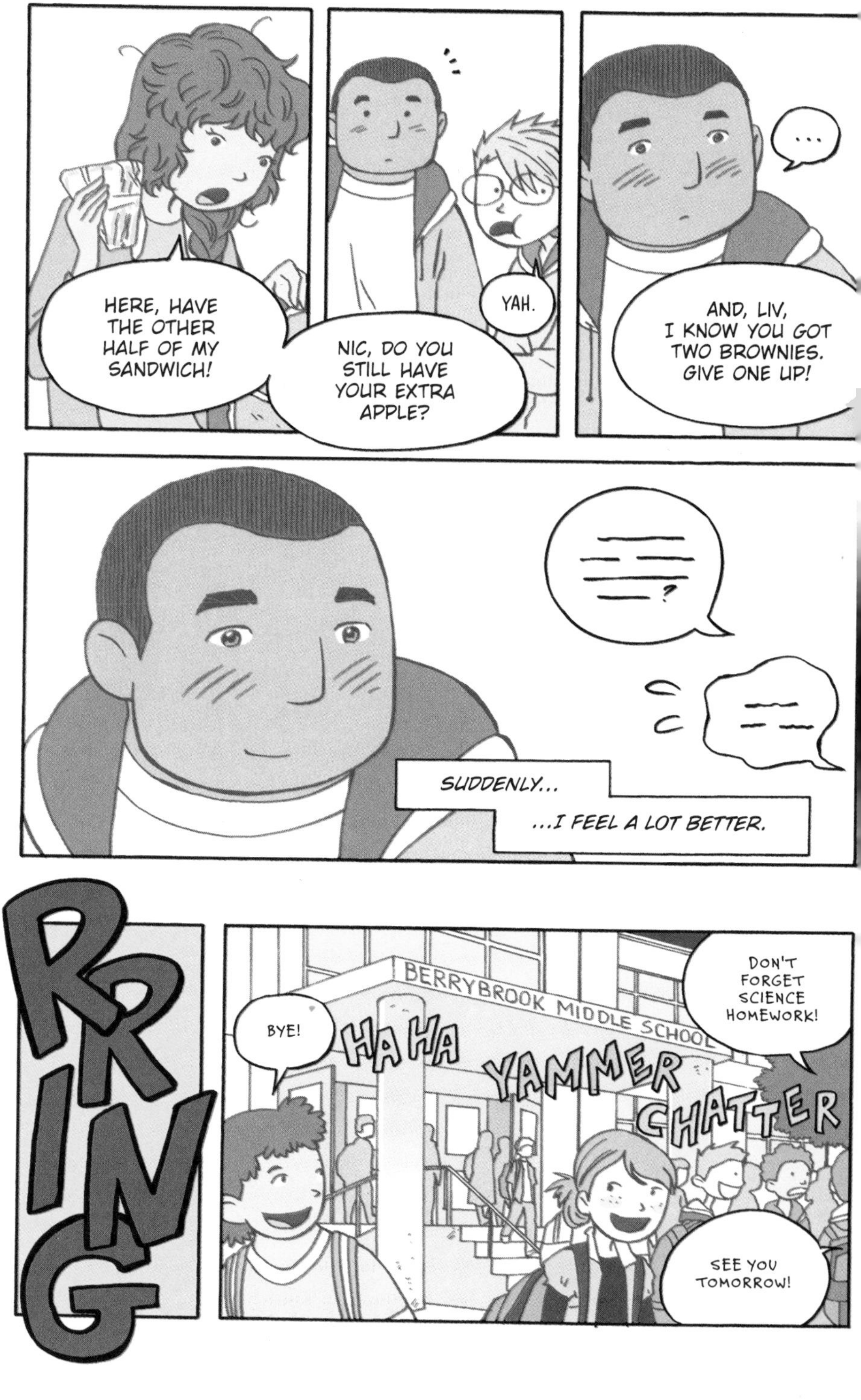
HERE, HAVE THE OTHER HALF OF MY SANDWICH!
NIC, DO YOU STILL HAVE YOUR EXTRA APPLE?
YAH.
...
AND, LIV, I KNOW YOU GOT TWO BROWNIES. GIVE ONE UP!
SUDDENLY...
...I FEEL A LOT BETTER.
RRING
BERRYBROOK MIDDLE SCHOOL
BYE!
HAHA
YAMMER
CHATTER
DON'T FORGET SCIENCE HOMEWORK!
SEE YOU TOMORROW!

THE BALL IS NEXT WEEK!! WHO'S EXCITED?!

SO SOON!

HA HA CHATTER HA

OOOOH! SHE'S GOT GOOD STUFF!

BRI, SO YOU'RE *NOT* WEARING A DRESS?

NOPE! CAN'T MAKE ME!

I AM! I'M STEALING MY SISTER'S.

I'M GETTING A HAIRCUT THIS WEEKEND.

OH! ME TOO!

ME THREE!

ME FOUR!

ME FIVE...

WHAAAT?! EVERYONE?

YOU GUYS, WE SHOULD HAVE A *HAIRCUT PARTY!!*

YESSSS.

OMG, I'D GO!

WHERE?

AT MY HOUSE! *BE THERE!*

YO, LIV, ARE WE INVITED?

OF COURSE!

HAHA

UH.

HAIRCUT PARTY?

I'M, UH... SKIPPING THAT.

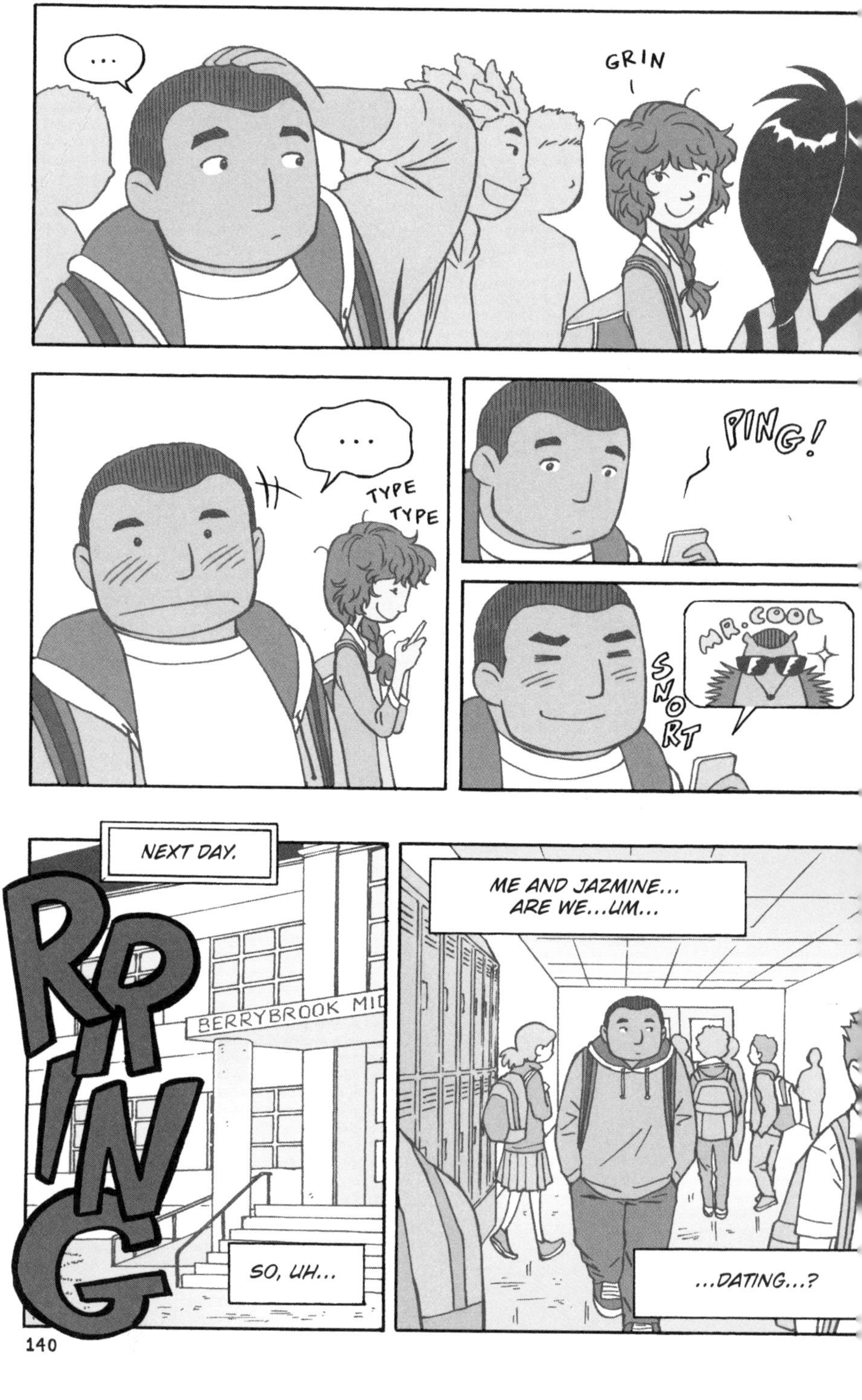

...
GRIN
...
TYPE TYPE
PING!
SNORT
MR. COOL
NEXT DAY.
RRING
BERRYBROOK MI
SO, UH...
ME AND JAZMINE... ARE WE...UM...
...DATING...?

I MEAN, WE TEXT, BUT... WE HAVEN'T REALLY...

...HUNG OUT. JUST THE TWO OF US.

THERE'S ALWAYS PEOPLE AROUND...

JORGE!!

....!

LIKE THAT.

LUNCH?

WE'RE EATING WITH THE DRAMA CREW AGAIN.

JAAAZMIIINE.

HEE-HEE!

YOU COMING?

. . .

I WANT TO, BUT...

OH.

UH.

ACTUALLY, I PROMISED I'D MEET GARRETT FOR LUNCH.

...WILL YOU COME?

UGH.

NO.

I'M NOT DONE BEING ANGRY AT HIM.

GIVE HIM A KICK IN THE SHINS FOR ME!

SEE YOU AT THE ATHLETICS MEET AFTER SCHOOL.

...

SEE YA!

...WISH THEY WOULD MAKE UP ALREADY.

HEY, SHRIMP-MAN.

IT'S COLD TODAY. YOU SURE YOU WANT TO EAT OUTSIDE?

OH YEAH, I JUST—

DON'T WANT JAMES TO SEE US.

...WHAT?

YOU EMBARRASSED OF ME OR SOMETHING?

WHAT?!

NO, NO!

IT'S JUST... JAMES GOT ALL WEIRD AND CRANKY WHEN I SAID I'M HAVING LUNCH WITH YOU.

....!

...THAT GUY'S **WEIRD**. WHY DO YOU HANG OUT WITH HIM?

WELL, WE'RE ON THE TEAM TOGETHER, AND...UH...

AND I'M FINALLY PART OF THE GROUP, Y'KNOW?

...

WELL, HE'S BEEN A REAL **JERK** LATELY.

HIM AND HIS CIRCUS MONKEYS.

....

...WHAT? N-NAW.

C'MON, THEY'RE JUST PLAYING.

JUST...KIDDING AROUND.

...

...

LOOK, I, UH—

H-HEY!

WHAT'S THIS I HEAR ABOUT YOU HAVING A GIRLFRIEND?

...

THAT CUTE CHICK FROM THE DRAMA CLUB, RIGHT?

...D-DON'T CALL HER "CHICK."

OH, WHOA, YOU'RE ALL RED!!

HA-HA! MUST BE SERIOUS!

DANG, AND HERE I THOUGHT WE'D BOTH BE BACHELORS AT THE BALL THING.

—ha ha

JAMES IS ON MY CASE TO GET A DATE...

EASY FOR *HIM* TO TALK. HE ALREADY HAS HIS DREAM DATE WITH *BROOKE*.

...

BROOKE?

...CRAP!!

I WASN'T SUPPOSED TO SAY THAT.

D-DON'T TELL ANYONE, OKAY? IT'S SUPPOSED TO BE THIS BIG *SECRET*.

...WHY?

UGH. JAMES WANTS THIS BIG REVEAL. LIKE THEY'RE CELEBRITIES OR SOMETHING.

HE WANTS EVERYONE TO BE IMPRESSED.

ESPECIALLY YOU.

ha ha

**WHAT.**

I'M SERIOUS!

HE WANTS YOU TO HANG WITH THEM SO BADLY.

...HOW COME YOU WON'T?

WINCE

...

I JUST DON'T LIKE THE GUY.

HE DOESN'T... RESPECT PEOPLE, Y'KNOW?

HE RESPECTS **YOU!** LIKE, A **LOT.**

HE'S ALWAYS "JORGE THIS" AND "JORGE THAT."

...UGH.

THAT'S NOT...

LIKE, I MEAN...

...

...HE'LL PUSH **ANYONE** AROUND IF HE CAN GET AWAY WITH IT.

JUST FOR FUNSIES.

...

AND HE'LL **LIE.**

AND GET OTHERS TO DO HIS DIRTY WORK SO **HE** DOESN'T GET IN TROUBLE.

I WORRY ABOUT YOU HANGING OUT WITH HIM, MAN.

...!

...

WATCH OUT, OKAY?

. . .

O-OKAY.

...

HEY, J, UH...

YEAH?

...DO YOU THINK LIV WILL GO TO THE BALL WITH ME?

...

...

WHAT?

WELL, I MEAN, SHE'S SINGLE NOW, SO...

...HE'S REALLY THAT CLUELESS.

UH.

I DUNNO.

MAYBE COME TO THE MEET TODAY AND ASK HER.

RRRING

OKAY, EVERYONE. SETTLE DOWN!!

...

...GUESS HE DIDN'T COME.

THIS IS OUR LAST GENERAL MEET BEFORE THE BALL!

LET'S MAKE IT COUNT!

OLIVIA, BROOKE.

I NEED YOU TO HAND THESE OUT TO EVERYONE, PLEASE.

NOW, FIRST THINGS FIRST—

YOU START ON THIS END. I'LL DO THE OTHER.

OKAY.

TAKE ONE AND PASS IT BACK.

CLAP CLAP CLAP

A BIG HAND FOR THE PLANNING COMMITTEE— YOU ARE ALL DOING AN AMAZING JOB!

THANK YOU.

SECOND—!

SCHOOL EVENT DRESS CODE! *LOOK IT UP.*

IT'S BEEN RECENTLY UPDATED AND IS IN YOUR STUDENT HANDBOOK.

WINK

WINK ♥

LET ME KNOW IF YOUR DOG ATE YOURS AND YOU NEED A NEW ONE.

HA HA HA HA

AND THIRD— *CODE OF CONDUCT.*

THERE WILL BE ONE AT THE BALL!

BROOKE AND OLIVIA ARE HANDING OUT THE PAPER COPIES, BUT YOU WILL ALSO GET AN E-MAIL.

RELATED TO THAT— REMEMBER HEALTH CLASS?

MORE SPECIFICALLY—

"BODY AUTONOMY"?

WHO CAN TELL ME WHAT THAT MEANS?

YES, BRIANNA?

IT MEANS MY BODY IS MINE AND NO ONE ELSE HAS A RIGHT TO IT.

THAT'S *RIGHT*.

AND THAT GOES FOR EVERYONE— BOYS, GIRLS, NONBINARY— YOUR BODY BELONGS TO *YOU*.

IF ANYONE'S TRYING TO TOUCH YOU WITHOUT YOUR CONSENT OR IGNORING A NO...

...THAT'S A *VIOLATION*.

WE WILL HAVE ADULT VOLUNTEERS AT THE DANCE, SO YOU CAN *REPORT* IT.

MORE DETAILS ARE IN THE HANDOUT...

...BUT THE SHORT OF IT IS—*RESPECT PERSONAL BOUNDARIES*. HAVE FUN THAT'S *NOT* AT THE EXPENSE OF SOMEONE ELSE.

...NOW, ON TO THE DECORATION DUTIES...

WE HAVE A SIGN-UP SHEET POSTED WITH THE—

CHATTER HA HA

HAIRCUT PARTY PEOPLE!

DON'T FORGET! MY HOUSE, TOMORROW! MAKE SURE YOU'RE PART OF THE GROUP CHAT!

J, YOU GONNA COME?

CHATTER ha ha ha

CAN'T. MY DAD'S TAKING ME TO THE GAME, REMEMBER?

OH YEAAAH!

WELL, DO YOU WANNA—

WHISPER SNICKER

C'mon, Ron.

OH, BRI, I LOVE YOUR BODY AUTONOMY!

WH-WHA...?

....!

HEY!! GET OFF HER!!

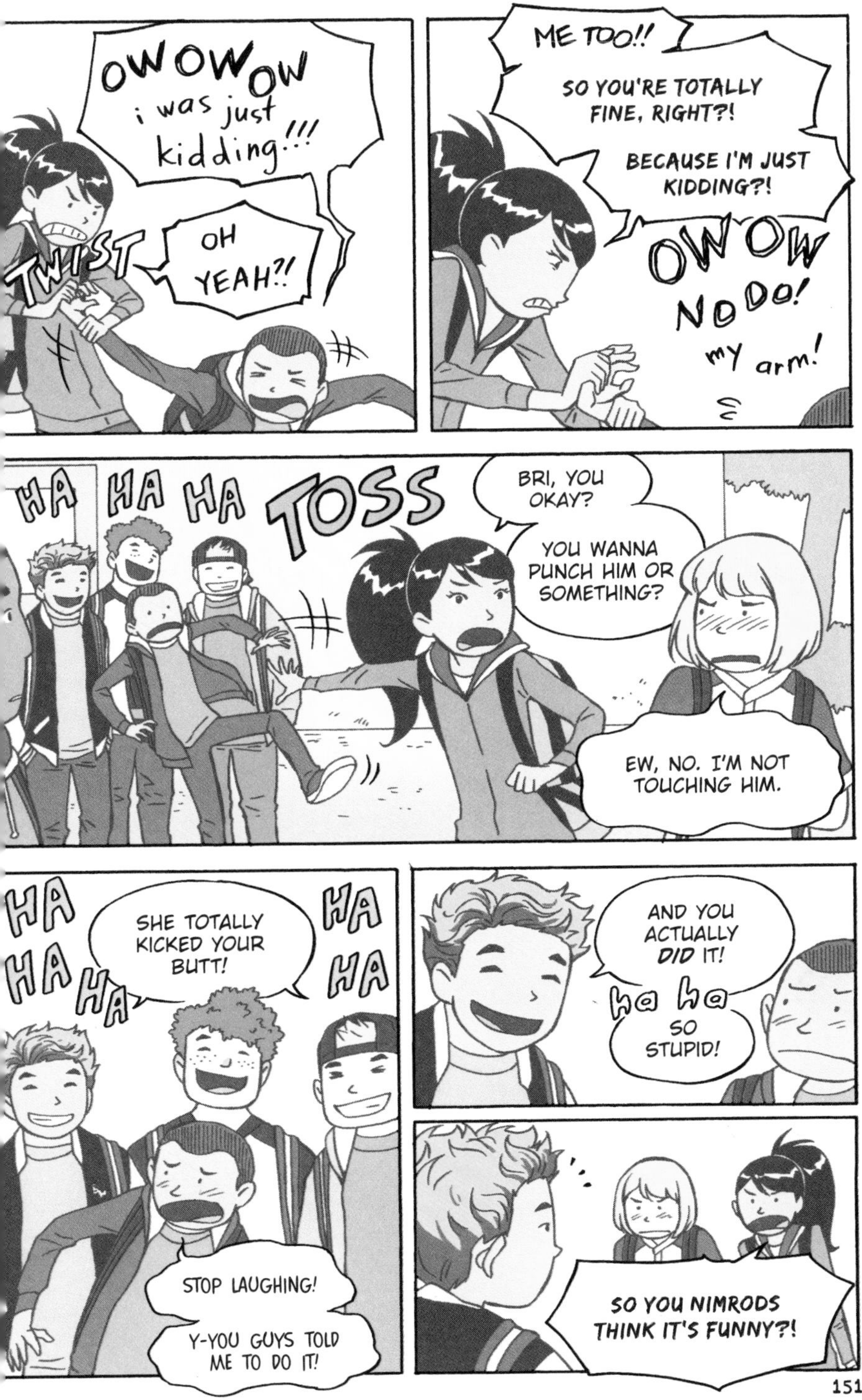
OWOWOWOW
i was just kidding!!!
TWIST
OH YEAH?!
ME TOO!!
SO YOU'RE TOTALLY FINE, RIGHT?!
BECAUSE I'M JUST KIDDING?!
OWOW NODO! my arm!
HA HA HA
TOSS
BRI, YOU OKAY?
YOU WANNA PUNCH HIM OR SOMETHING?
EW, NO. I'M NOT TOUCHING HIM.
HA HA HA
SHE TOTALLY KICKED YOUR BUTT!
HA HA
STOP LAUGHING!
Y-YOU GUYS TOLD ME TO DO IT!
AND YOU ACTUALLY DID IT!
ha ha
SO STUPID!
SO YOU NIMRODS THINK IT'S FUNNY?!

...!

YOU INCITED ASSAULT!

YOU WANNA TELL THIS TO MRS. RASHAD AND SEE HOW MUCH SHE LAUGHS?!

WH-WHOA, HEY, NOW.

WE'RE SORRY.

WON'T DO IT AGAIN, I PROMISE.

Y-YEAH.

OK.

YEP.

EVERYONE'S GONNA BE GOOD AND RESPECTFUL, RIGHT, GUYS?

...

YEAH, YOU BETTER.

CREEPS.

WINK

...!

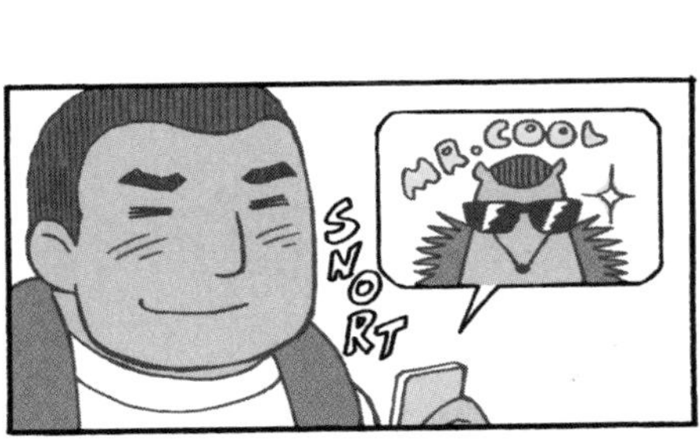
SNORT
MR. COOL

# CHAPTER 8

MONDAY.

RRRING

...THAT "CODE OF CONDUCT" THING WAS MISSING SOME PRETTY IMPORTANT STUFF.

LUNCH? OUTSIDE?

HEY, WAIT UP!

I MEAN, I GET THE "DON'T BE A GRABBY JERK" PART, BUT...

...WHAT ABOUT THE OTHER STUFF? LIKE...SH-SHOULD I GET A GIFT?

FLOWERS?

CHOCOLATE?

HISS    HISS

a hedgehog...?

A-A CORSAGE?

...OR IS THAT ONLY FOR PROMS...?

...NOW I WISH I STAYED AWAKE FOR ALL THOSE DUMB ROMANCE MOVIES LIV MADE US WATCH.

MAKE IT STAAAHP! KISS! KISS!

....!

LIV!

YO, LIV, I GOT A QUES—

JORGE! WHAT'S UP?

—TION.

...

Y-YOUR... YOUR HAIR...

OLIVIA HOFFMAN, 13 Y.O. HAIR = **CUT**

WHAT'S WITH THAT REACTION?! YOU'VE SEEN MY HAIR SHORT BEFORE!

SLAP

YEAH...

WHEN YOU WERE, LIKE, **SIX**.

HA HA

WELL, GET USED TO IT!

I LOVE IT SHORT. I CAN'T BELIEVE I WAITED SO LONG.

...WHAT WAS YOUR QUESTION?

OH! YEAH.

I WAS GONNA ASK ABOUT, UH—

LIV! JORGE! YOU GUYS GOING TO LUNCH?

...!

BROOKE?

BROOKE BENSON, 13 Y.O. HAIR = ALSO CUT

HELLOOO, JORGE! DON'T YOU RECOGNIZE ME?

Hiii.

I THINK HE MIGHT BE IN SHOCK.

IT JUST LOOKS REAL DIFFERENT.

I LOVE HOW LIGHT IT FEELS!

TOSS

I KNOW, RIGHT?

OH, AND THE BEST PART?! IT WAS FOR CHARITY!

WE WERE JUST GONNA GET REGULAR CUTS, BUT THE SALON WAS HAVING THIS CHARITY DRIVE—

!

YEAH!

THEY MAKE WIGS FOR SICK KIDS WHO CAN'T AFFORD THEM!

...!

THAT'S... COOL.

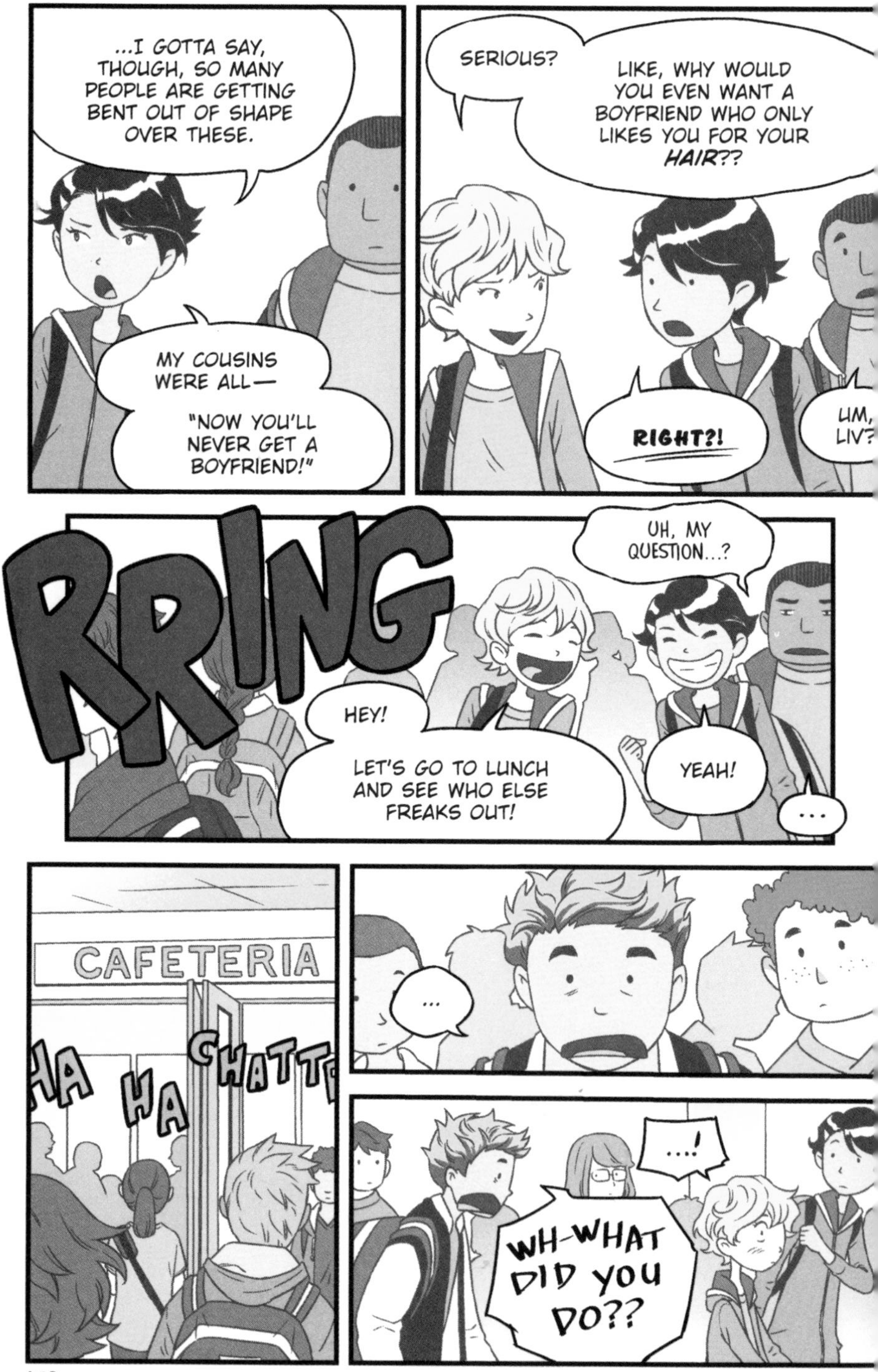
...I GOTTA SAY, THOUGH, SO MANY PEOPLE ARE GETTING BENT OUT OF SHAPE OVER THESE.
MY COUSINS WERE ALL—
"NOW YOU'LL NEVER GET A BOYFRIEND!"
SERIOUS?
LIKE, WHY WOULD YOU EVEN WANT A BOYFRIEND WHO ONLY LIKES YOU FOR YOUR *HAIR*??
RIGHT?!
UM, LIV?
RRING
UH, MY QUESTION...?
HEY!
LET'S GO TO LUNCH AND SEE WHO ELSE FREAKS OUT!
YEAH!
...
CAFETERIA
HA
HA
CHATTE
...
...!
WH-WHAT DID YOU DO??

H-HUH?

Y-YOUR HAIR...?

...OH!

WE CUT IT FOR CHARITY! CUTE, HUH?

...

WHA—?

...THE BALL IS THIS FRIDAY!!

ARE YOU GOING... LOOKING LIKE *THAT*?

E-EXCUSE ME...?

LOOKING LIKE *WHAT*?

...!

LIKE...

LIKE A *JOKE*!

...*EXCUSE you*?!

I-I MEAN, YOU WERE SO *PRETTY* BEFORE!

I STILL AM!!

...BUT YOUR *HAIR*...!

ARE YOU SERIO—

...WAAAIT.

...DID YOU ASK ME OUT *JUST* BECAUSE I'M PRETTY?

....!

WELL, UH.

UM...

OMG, YOU DID!

EWWWW!

W-WAIT, UH.

I THOUGHT YOU ACTUALLY *LIKED* ME! I DON'T BELIEVE THIS!

...I DON'T DATE SHALLOW TRASH BAGS.

GO TO THE BALL BY YOURSELF.

....!

... WHAT—?

SHE THINKS YOU'RE GROSS, JAMES. I DO TOO.

BROOKE, WAIT UP.

WHAT?! WHAT DID I DO?!

...

UH.

BYE.

...WHAT IS HAPPENING TO EVERYONE THIS YEAR?!

DRAMA **EVERYWHERE!!**

THERE'S NO ESCAPE!

NEVER THOUGHT I'D MISS THIRD GRADE...

...WHEN WE ALL JUST HUNG OUT...

SIGH

UM, JORGE?

JAZMINE?

H-HI.

161

JAZMINE DUONG, 13 Y.O.

. . .

UM.

I JUST WANTED TO MAKE SURE...

...YOU HAVE YOUR LUNCH?

I HAVE LOTS OF FOOD I CAN SHARE...

... UH.

I GOT MY FOOD.

I'M OKAY.

OH. OKAY, COOL.

S-SEE YOU LATER.

....!

W-WAIT!

....?

...

D-DO YOU WANNA...

...GO EAT OUTSIDE?

...IT HAPPENED AGAIN.

...I-I JUST BLURTED THAT OUT.

AND SHE SAID YES!

...EXCEPT NOW, I DON'T KNOW WHAT TO SAY.

...

UH.

YOU SURE YOU DON'T WANT TO TRY SOME OF MY FOOD?

163

UH. N-NAW, I'M OKAY.

I GOT MY SANDWICH.

R-R STL

OH. OKAY.

...

...

...MAYBE I SHOULD'VE SAID YES?

THIS IS SO AWKWARD.

...

...

...

...THEIR PLAY! YESSSS, I CAN ASK ABOUT—

...Um, by the way...

Y-YEAH?

I'M, UM...

...REAL GLAD YOU DIDN'T FREAK OUT ABOUT MY HAIR.

SOME OTHER PEOPLE HAVE...

....!

I-IT'S YOUR HAIR.

THAT... THAT BODY AUTONOMY THING, RIGHT?

IT'S YOUR DECISION.

AND...AND LIV SAID IT'S HELPING SICK KIDS?

YEAH!

THAT'S REAL COOL OF YOU.

...

WELL, MY MOM'S BEEN SICK...

...AND SOME OF THE TREATMENTS MADE HER LOSE HER HAIR, SO SHE WORE WIGS...

I KNOW IT WAS ROUGH ON HER. I CAN'T EVEN IMAGINE HOW IT IS FOR A KID.

...YOUR MOM'S SICK?

...

UM, YEAH.

...BUT SHE'S GETTING BETTER!

SHE'S GOING TO COME TO OUR PLAY.

...OH! SPEAKING OF WHICH!

WE NEED TO SELL TICKETS TOO!

!

DO YOU THINK YOU GUYS CAN HELP?

RELATIVES, FRIENDS, ENEMIES?

WE NEED WARM BODIES. WE'LL TAKE *ANYONE*.

HA-HA, OH YEAH.

LIV AND I WILL GET YOU *PEOPLE*.

ha ha ha

I KNOW, RIGHT?

...OH, OH, AND MR. KRISTOFFER!

IT'S LIKE HE'S OUT TO RUIN EVERY STUDENT'S LIFE WITH *MATH*!

HA-HA! DEF A CONSPIRACY.

MISS TOBINS IS MY FAVORITE.

I MEAN, SHE'S TERRIFYING, BUT I LOVE THE—

...THIS IS GOING SO WELL.

DON'T KNOW WHY I WAS WORRIED. I GOT THIS.

...

WELL, TIME FOR CLASS, I GUESS...

...NOOOO!

WAH, I HAVE GEOGRAPHY NEXT...

...I WISH WE HAD CLASSES TOGETHER.

UM. I'LL TEXT YOU?

Y-YEAH.

BYE!

BY—

...

!

IS THAT... ...ZEKE?

WELL, WELL, *WELL.*

*HELLO* THERE. FINALLY.

GUH!

Z-ZEKE!

I SEE, I SEE.

I GET IT NOW.

...!

YOU GET *WHAT?*

WHY YOU BROKE UP WITH ME!

WHY SETTLE FOR ME WHEN YOU CAN UPGRADE TO A JOCK, RIGHT?

...!

WHAT?

!! !!

...

WELL, JUST FYI, YOU WEREN'T THAT GOOD A GIRLFRIEND ANYWAY!!

...AND YOUR NEW HAIRCUT SUCKS!

...!

THIS, GUY.

HEY, ZEKE, COME BACK HERE—

...WHAT? NO!

I DON'T WANT HIM TO COME BACK!

BUT...H-HE SHOULDN'T SAY THAT STUFF ABOUT YOU...!

NO.

BUT IF I BEAT HIM UP, I'D GET IN TROUBLE.

YOU WOULD TOO.

...!

AND HE'S SO NOT WORTH IT. TRUST ME.

...

—IF I BEAT HIM UP—

THAT'S...KINDA BADASS.

I'LL TEXT YOU, OKAY?

...

Y-YEAH.

IT'S OFFICIAL.

...I'M TAKING THE AWESOMEST GIRL IN SCHOOL TO THE BALL.

FRIDAY NIGHT.

HAHA

YAMMER CHATTER

AD ASTRA

WELCOME ATHLETE

HA HA

HEY SMILE!

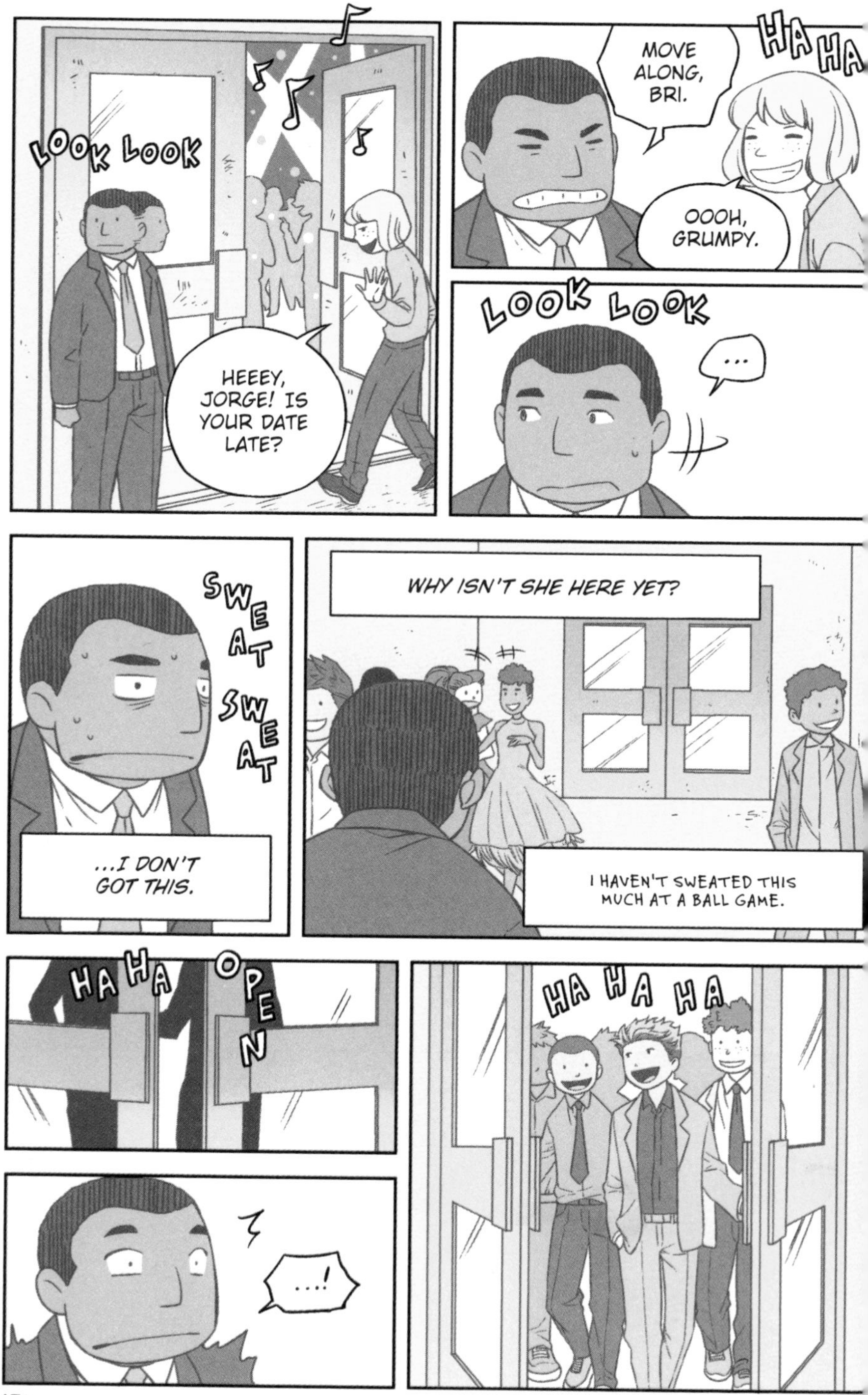
LOOK LOOK
HEEEY, JORGE! IS YOUR DATE LATE?
MOVE ALONG, BRI.
HAHA
OOOH, GRUMPY.
LOOK LOOK
...
SWEAT SWEAT
...I DON'T GOT THIS.
WHY ISN'T SHE HERE YET?
I HAVEN'T SWEATED THIS MUCH AT A BALL GAME.
HAHA
OPEN
...!
HA HA HA HA

...IT'S JUST JAMES AND HIS GOONS.

...HE'S PROBABLY GONNA TRY TO TALK TO ME AGAIN.

UGH.

...

...!

...WOW. WHAT WAS *THAT* LOOK?

...OR NOT.

JORGE, H-HEY!

GARRETT!

HEY, MAN.

UH.

...!

WHAT'S UP WITH JAMES?

OH, UH. S-SORRY, I—

I ACCIDENTALLY TOLD HIM WHY YOU WOULDN'T HANG OUT... sorry...

171

**WHAT?!** DUDE, THAT WAS *PRIVATE!*

I KNOW, I KNOW, I'M SORRY!

HE KEPT PUSHING ME, ASKING!

UUGH.

BUT HEY, NOW HE'LL STOP BUGGING YOU TO HANG OUT?

... TRUE.

...

H-HEY, UM.

C-CAN I COME OVER TOMORROW?

PLAY, LIKE BEFORE?

...I MISS HANGING OUT WITH YOU.

... WHAT ABOUT JAMES?

OH, I'LL... MAKE SOMETHING UP.

HE WON'T EVEN KNOW.

...UH. OKAY, SURE.

YESSS!

DO YOU THINK LIV WOULD CO—

**HEY, GARRETT!**

JAMES, YO! I WAS JUST—

ARE YOU PART OF THE TEAM TONIGHT OR WHAT?

Y-YEAH, FOR SURE!

THEN MOVE IT OR LOSE YOUR SPOT!

YEAH. YEAH, I WAS JUST...

HA HA

OPEN

...

!

HA HA HA HA

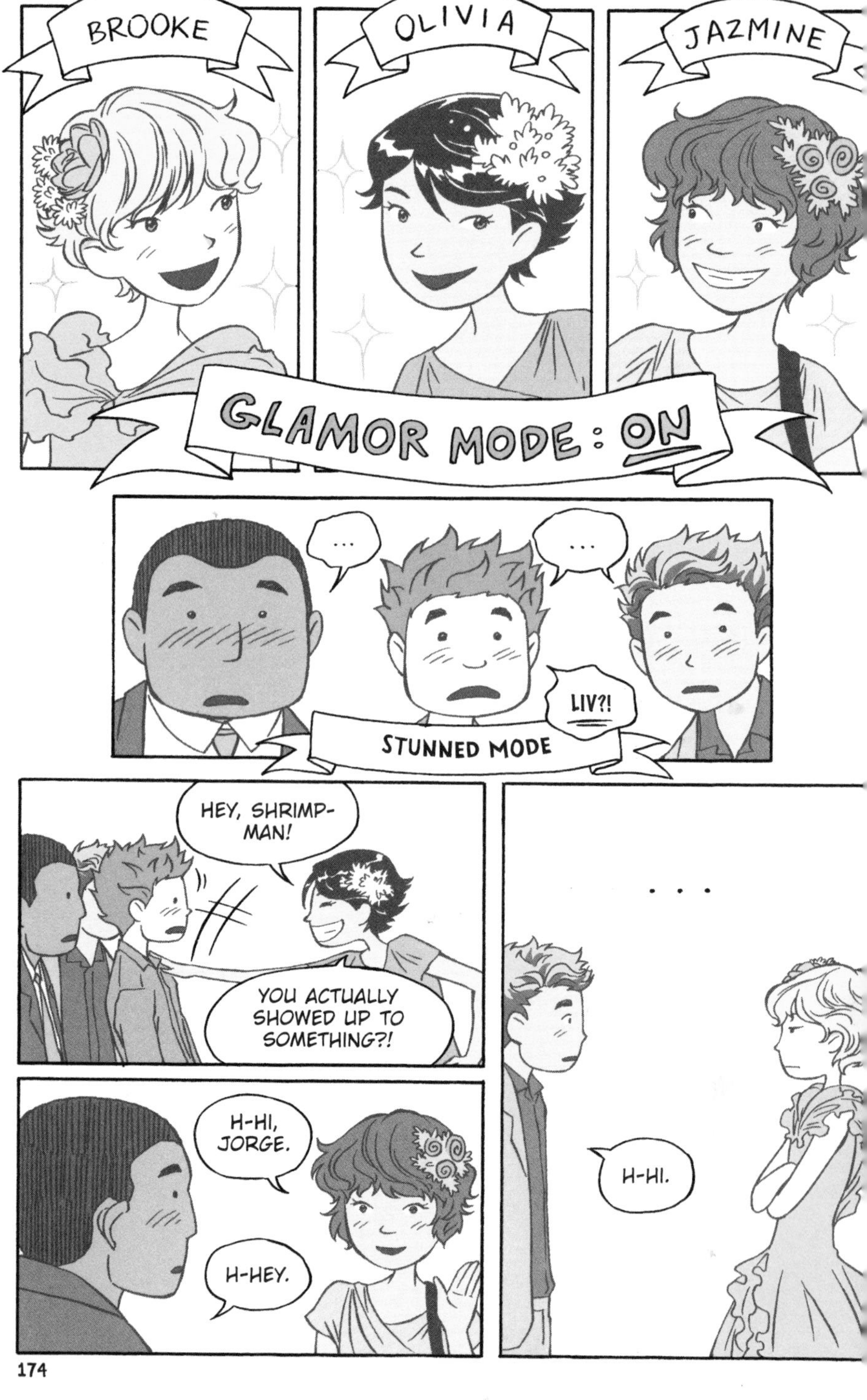
BROOKE
OLIVIA
JAZMINE
GLAMOR MODE: ON
...
...
LIV?!
STUNNED MODE
HEY, SHRIMP-MAN!
YOU ACTUALLY SHOWED UP TO SOMETHING?!
H-HI, JORGE.
H-HEY.
...
H-HI.

HMPF!

C'MON, GARRETT, MOVE IT.

STOMP STOMP STOMP

U-UH.

GOTTA GO.

...

BRI! HEY!

...

Y-YOU LOOK AMAZING.

TH-THANKS.

...MY HEAD IS COMPLETELY BLANK.

COME ON, YOU WALLFLOWERS!!

WAH!

IT'S PARTY TIME!!

DRAG

...THANK GOD FOR LIV.

TURNS OUT, I WAS NERVOUS FOR NO REASON.

WELCOME, EVERYONE, TO THE ANNUAL ATHLETICS FUND-RAISER BALL!

FIRST, LET'S GIVE A BIG HAND TO THE PLANNING COMMITTEE FOR THEIR—

CLAP

CLAP

CLAP

CLAP

CLAP

THE DJ ONLY HAD ONE SETTING—*VERY LOUD.*

SO TALKING?

TOTALLY **OPTIONAL.**

I CAN'T HEAR YOU!!

WHAT?!

HERE FOR THIS.

THE DRAMA CLUB DID A MADE-UP SPORTS TRIVIA COMEDY SHOW...

...AND THERE WERE GAMES WITH PRIZES...

MRS. RASHAD'S HUSBAND AND MRS. FERRIS'S WIFE TRIED TO WIN THE SAME STUFFED TOY.

TOSS

RAZZA-FRAZZIN'...

FIGHT! WIN! ♥

I'LL LOVE YOU EITHER WAY!

BUT PLEASE WIN! ♥

...AND THEN LIV WON IT. BECAUSE OF COURSE.

YESSSS!

YAY! ha ha

CLAP CLAP

CHAMPION

ALMOST EVERYONE HAD A BALL. (HEH.)

...

ALMOST.

AW, THE DANCING'S STARTING!

CAN WE AT LEAST DANCE?

IF YOU WANT TO LOOK *STUPID.*

...

HEY, SHRIMP-MAN!

I'M DONE BEING ANGRY AT YOU!

WANNA COME DANCE WITH US?

NO, HE DOESN'T. SHOO.

GRAB

YEAAAH, LET'S GO!

...

LOOK WHO IIIII FOUND!

GARRETT!!

HI!

I'M NOT MUCH OF A PARTY PERSON...OR A DANCE PERSON...

...BUT SOMEHOW, EVERYTHING WAS TEN TIMES MORE FUN TODAY.

OMG, I LOVE THIS SONG!

WITH HER.

BERRYBROOK MIDDLE SCHOOL

BYE.

SEE YA!

OH, THERE'S MY PARENTS' CAR.

OH, OKAY.

S-SORRY I HAVE TO LEAVE SO EARLY...

STUPID CURFEW.

IT'S COOL.

. . .

UM. WELL...

...I REALLY NEED TO SAY SOMETHING RIGHT NOW.

THANKS FOR INVITING ME.

I HAD A REALLY FUN TIME.

OH! GOOD.

M-ME T—

PECK ♥

!

OH NO!

I'M SO SORRY! I SHOULD'VE ASKED FIRST!

WH-WHA...?

NO, NO, YOU'RE GOOD.

Y-YOU...

YOU NEVER HAVE TO ASK.

*OTHER* PEOPLE BETTER ASK.

BUT NOT YOU.

...

okay.

I'LL TEXT YOU!

DASH

O-OKAY!

LIFE...

...IS **SO** GOOD RIGHT NOW.

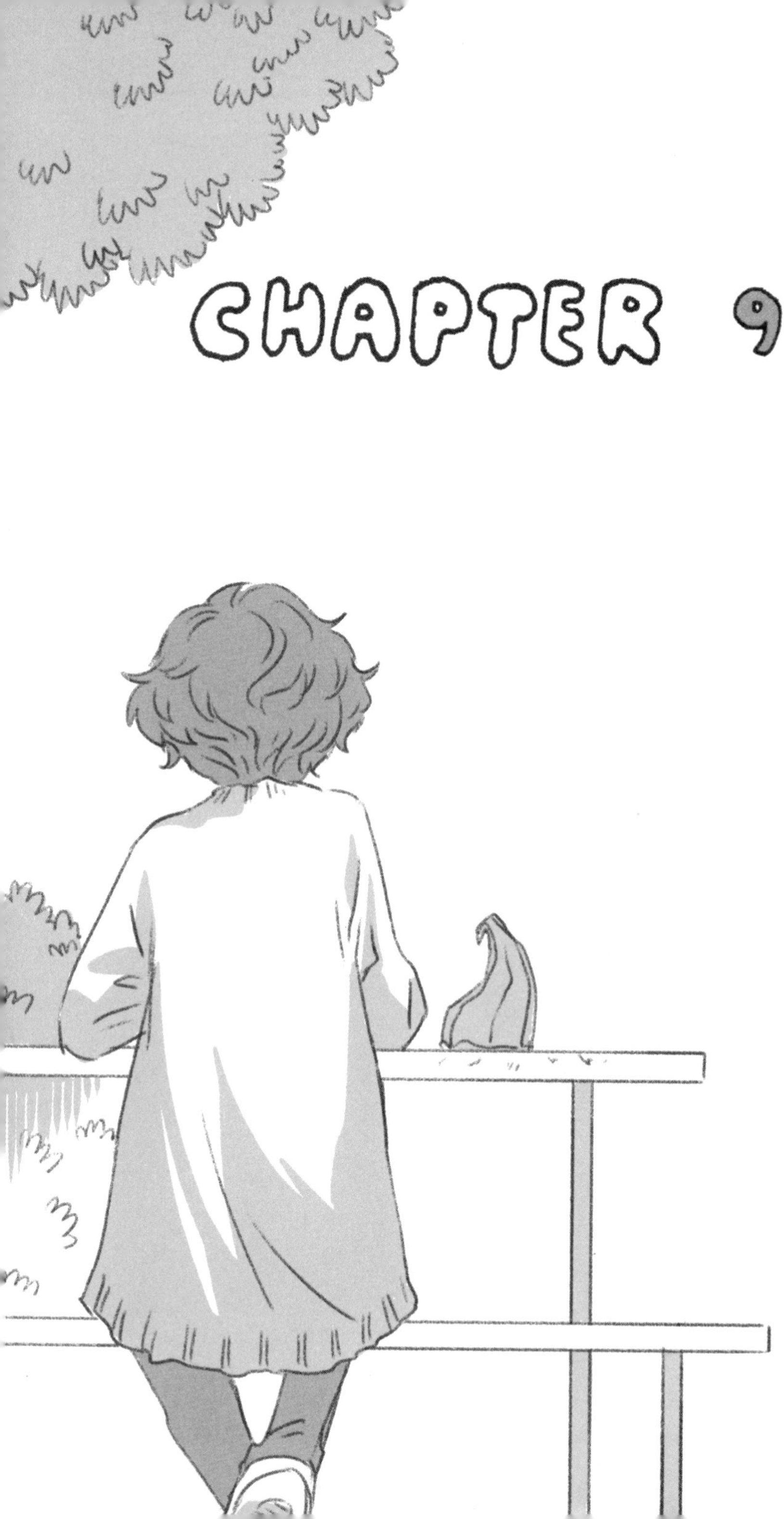
CHAPTER 9

MONDAY.

I HAVEN'T BEEN THIS EXCITED ABOUT A MONDAY SINCE...

...UH.

• • •

...OKAY, I'VE NEVER BEEN EXCITED ABOUT A MONDAY, BUT WHATEVER.

I HAD THE **BEST** WEEKEND.

FRIDAY WAS AMAZING FOR OBVIOUS REASONS...

...AND THEN GARRETT CAME OVER TO HANG OUT ON SATURDAY, AND IT WAS JUST LIKE OLD TIMES.

HE DID GET A BIT WEIRD AT THE END...LIKE HE WAS AFRAID JAMES MIGHT FIND OUT...

....!

HEY, MAN!

DIDN'T SEE YOU ON THE BUS AGAIN TODAY.

SLAM

O-OH, UM.

Y-YEAH, I...

UM, I GOTTA GO.

...!

...BUT HE'LL COME AROUND... RIGHT?

...

WHISPER    WHISPER
...jorge did...?
are you sure?
oops, there he is.

...!

!! *SCATTER*

uh, let's go...

...?

...

...BUT ANYWAY...

ON SUNDAY, JAZMINE AND I KEPT TEXTING FOREVER.

WE'RE GONNA HAVE LUNCH TOGETHER AGAIN TODA—

YOU'RE SUCH A TWO-FACE, JORGE RUIZ.

...?!

WH-WHA—?

YOU'RE ALL NICE TO MY FACE AND THEN TALK TRASH ABOUT ME BEHIND MY BACK?!

H-HUH?

WHAT ARE YOU TALKING ABOUT...?

YOU CAN DROP THE NICE GUY ACT, OKAY?

I SAW THE CHAT SCREENSHOTS!

THE WHA—?

YOU CALLED ME AN UGLY DOG!

NEVER TALK TO ME AGAIN!

WHISPER

really?

...

WHISPER

...him....?

...WH-WHAT? WHAT'S GOING ON?

RRING

LUNCH.

WHISPER WHISPER

...

TIC TOC

...

TIC TOC

... ...

TIC TOC

...?

SH-SHE IS COMING, RIGHT?

SHE WOULDN'T...

...STAND ME UP...?

JORGE!!

HUFF HUFF

...LIV?

WHAT—?

DID SOMEONE HACK YOUR SCHOOL CHAT ACCOUNT?

WH-WHA...?

LIV'S REALLY GOOD AT EXPLAINING.

BUT I STILL COULDN'T GET IT AT FIRST.

IT JUST SOUNDED SO...LIKE, I WAS GETTING PRANKED?

LIKE, NOT BELIEVABLE.

WAIT, WAIT...

SCREENSHOTS?

OF A CHAT?

THAT I WAS IN?

NOT *YOU*!

SOMEONE *ELSE*, USING *YOUR* HANDLE!

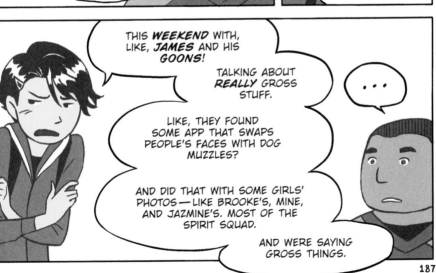

THIS **WEEKEND** WITH, LIKE, **JAMES** AND HIS **GOONS**!

TALKING ABOUT **REALLY** GROSS STUFF.

LIKE, THEY FOUND SOME APP THAT SWAPS PEOPLE'S FACES WITH DOG MUZZLES?

AND DID THAT WITH SOME GIRLS' PHOTOS—LIKE BROOKE'S, MINE, AND JAZMINE'S. MOST OF THE SPIRIT SQUAD.

AND WERE SAYING GROSS THINGS.

...

187

...AND WHOEVER WAS USING YOUR ACCOUNT, THEY WERE ALL, "OH, THOSE ARE UGLY DOGS, LOL!"

"SOMEONE TAKE THEM TO THE POUND, LOL, LOL!"

...AND THEN, SOMEONE SCREENCAPPED IT AND POSTED IT ONLINE!!

SO NOW PEOPLE THINK YOU WERE IN THAT RUDE CHAT!!

• • •

BUT...

...I *WASN'T*.

**I KNOW!!**

**YOU'D NEVER SAY THAT STUFF!**

W-WAIT...

...IS THAT WHY...

...EVERYONE'S BEEN WHISPERING...AND BROOKE WAS—

WHISPER

WHISPER

...!

188

B-BUT IT WASN'T ME!

I *KNOW!*

SOMEONE MUST'VE HACKED YOU!

...no. no, no, no.

is that why she didn't come?

WHO?

JAZMINE.

WE WERE SUPPOSED TO EAT LUNCH TOGETHER.

D-DOES SHE THINK I—

...!

IF SHE DOES, SHE'S GONNA STOP, OKAY?!

I'LL GO FIND HER!

YOU THINK ABOUT WHO MIGHT WANT TO HACK YOU!

...!

...

JAMES.

WELL, WELL, WELL.

IT'S MISTER TOO-GOOD-TO-HANG-OUT-WITH-US!

...!

NICE HAVING YOU IN OUR *CHAT* THIS WEEKEND.

HEH HEH

YOU KNOW THAT WASN'T ME!!

DO I?

IT *LOOKED* LIKE YOU.

RIGHT, GUYS?

IT WAS TOTALLY JORGE, THE GOODY TWO-SHOES, YEAH?

...

IT WAS OBVIOUS **WHAT** THEY KNEW.

...

...

...

AND THEY WOULDN'T SAY ANYTHING TO HELP ME.

R R I N G

ENGLISH CLASS.

YOU **SUCK.**

WH-WHA...?

J-JAZMINE IS OUR FRIEND!

WE THOUGHT YOU **LIKED** HER!

WE SAW THE CHAT SCREENS! H-HOW COULD YOU **SAY** THAT GROSS STUFF ABOUT HER AND LET **THEM** SAY IT?!

YEAH!

**AND** LAUGH ABOUT IT?

...

BUT... BUT I DIDN'T...

I-IT WASN'T ME!

191

RIGHT.

IT WAS SOME OTHER JORGE RUIZ?

....!

L-LOOK.

IT WAS...

...I WAS *HACKED!*

SERIOUSLY?

YOU THINK WE'D BUY THAT?

H-HEY!

S-STOP HARASSING HIM.

....!

I-IF HE SAYS IT WASN'T HIM, THEN THAT'S *TRUE!*

NOD NOD

J-JORGE IS A *GOOD* PERSON.

WOULD A "GOOD PERSON" MAKE HIS GIRLFRIEND CRY?!

...

JAZMINE WAS CRYING ALL MORNING!

NO, NO, NO, NO!!

I HAVE TO FIND HER!

DRAMA CLUB.

WHAT DO YOU WANT?

U-UH.

JAZMINE?

I NEED TO... TELL HER...

OH, I THINK YOU'VE SAID *ENOUGH.*

SHE'S NOT HERE. GO AWAY!

JERK!

SLAM

...MAYBE...

MAYBE SHE'S HIDING NEAR THAT BACK DOOR AGAIN...?

LIKE LAST TIME?

...AFTER ZEKE.

...

JAZ—

KTK

...!

GARRETT!!

YOU GOTTA HELP ME!

...

DO YOU KNOW HOW JAMES GOT AHOLD OF MY ACCOUNT AND POSTED ALL THAT?!

...

I-it...

It wasn't James.

HUH?

THEN WHO WAS IT?

...

M-me.

...

WH-WHAT?

I...I didn't mean to!

I...

I was at your place, on Saturday, when James...

He was all, "get in the chat now or else!"

...S-so I did...

...from your laptop...

...I thought I logged out!!

But then...it was still your account...

I didn't know they'd be taking screenshots!

. . .

K T K

...HA!

**THOUGHT** YOU MIGHT TRY TO SNEAK OUT THE BACK DOOR.

SO, LOOKS LIKE YOU KNOW, HUH?

WHAT DO YOU THINK OF YOUR BEST BUDDY NOW?

PRETTY SPINELESS, HUH?

PU SH

Y-YOU...!

WHY'D YOU DO IT? WHY'D YOU POST THE SCREENSHOTS?

YO, I DID **NOT** POST THOSE. DO YOU THINK I'M **STUPID**?

MY NAME'S IN THERE!

I DON'T KNOW WHO DID IT...

...BUT WHEN I FIND THEM, THEY'RE GONNA BE **SORRY**.

...

I BETTER NOT GET SUSPENDED FROM THE TEAM FOR THIS...

...

BUT, HEY!

WOULDN'T WANNA BE **YOU** RIGHT NOW, THOUGH!

HA HA

WHAT ARE YOU GONNA DO?

...

RAT OUT YOUR FRIEND TO THE WHOLE SCHOOL SO EVERYONE HATES **HIM** INSTEAD?

...!

LOYAL, TOO-GOOD-FOR-THIS-WORLD JORGE...

...TELLING ON HIS FRIEND TO SAVE HIS OWN SKIN...

YOU'LL HAVE TO!

'COS *HE'S* NEVER GONNA TELL. HE'S NOT *STUPID.*

...

RIGHT, G?

PUSH

LEAVE ME ALONE!!

DASH

HA HA HA

I'M SURE HE'S RUSHING TO TELL EVERYONE!

ha ha

ha ha ha

SHOULD'VE PICKED BETTER FRIENDS, SHERIFF!

GOOD *LUCK.*

HA HA HA

...

# CHAPTER 10

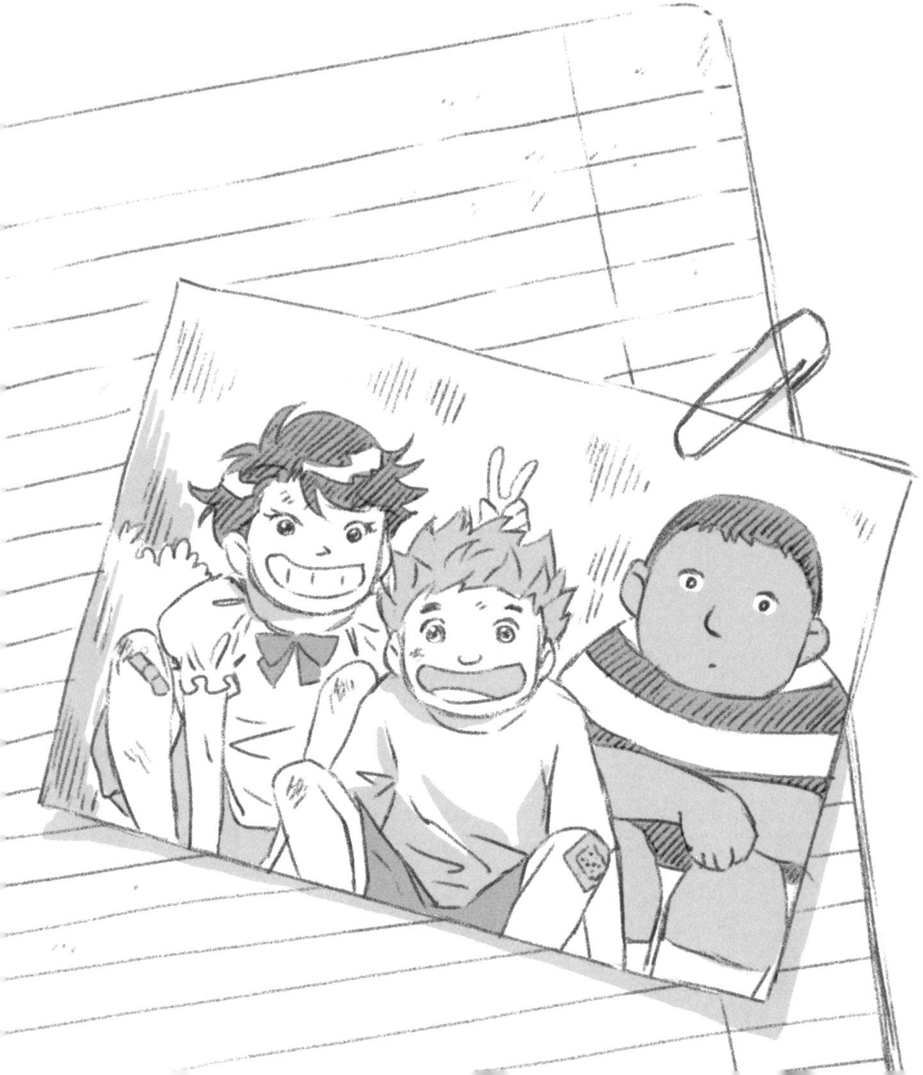

NEXT DAY, LUNCH.

...SO, WAIT, IT MIGHT NOT HAVE BEEN HIM?

NAW, HE'S ALL NICE TO YOUR FACE BUT WILL TALK CRAP ABOUT YOU ONLINE.

THAT'S NOT TRUE!

GOSSIP

GOSSIP

MAYBE IT WAS PHOTOSHOPPED?

I DON'T EVEN KNOW.

...I HEARD HE GOT HACKED...

THAT'S WHAT HE'D *LIKE* YOU TO THINK.

...JAMES, THOUGH, *WOW*. AM I RIGHT?

...

*UGH*, YEAH. WHAT A JERK.

I HATE THIS.

GOSSIP YAMMER

...

PEOPLE ARE TOO AFRAID TO COME AT ME, BUT THEY GOSSIP AND GIVE ME DIRTY LOOKS.

AND THERE WAS A BUNCH OF NASTY NOTES SHOVED IN MY LOCKER TODAY.

...JAZMINE PROBABLY HATES ME.

I DIDN'T EVEN DO ANYTHING!

i-it was me...

i-i didn't mean to!

I TRIED CALLING GARRETT SEVERAL TIMES YESTERDAY...

HIS MOM SAID HE WAS SUPER SICK, LIKE THROWING UP ALL THE TIME.

HE'S NOT EVEN IN SCHOOL TODAY.

GOSSIP GOSSIP YAMMER

...SO I'M DEALING WITH THIS ON MY OWN, I GUESS.

?

....J-JORGE?

....!

J-JAZMINE!

...

U-UM.

L-LIV SAID...

...THAT WASN'T REALLY YOU?

IN...

IN THAT HORRIBLE CHAT?

....!

NO!

I WOULD NEVER SAY THAT STUFF!

ABOUT *ANYONE!*

...E-ESPECIALLY YOU.

O-OH.

...GOOD.

HE *REALLY* WOULDN'T! EVER!

JORGE'S GOOD PEOPLE!

...HE JUST GOT HACKED BY SOME JERK TRYING TO MAKE HIM LOOK BAD.

WE'RE STILL FIGURING OUT WHO IT WAS.

...JORGE, DID YOU THINK OF ANYONE IT COULD'VE BEEN?

...

...

...JORGE?

...

I *CANNOT* TELL HER. SHE'LL HATE HIM FOREVER.

...BUT I ALSO CAN'T LIE TO HER WORTH BEANS.

...JORGE?

...UH.

...WAIT.

DO YOU...

...*KNOW* WHO IT WAS?

LOOOM

UM.

OMG, YOU DO KNOW!!

WHY ARE YOU KEEPING QUIET?!

WHO WAS IT?! TELL ME!!

NO, I CAN'T.

...

ARE YOU ACTUALLY PROTECTING THEM? STOP BEING SO NICE!

THEY'RE HANGING YOU OUT TO DRY!!

UUGH!

FINE! I'M GONNA FIND THIS SACK OF WEASELS MYSELF, THEN!

...YOU SAID ZEKE SENT YOU THOSE SCREENSHOTS, RIGHT?

Y-YEAH...

HE WAS SO SMARMY ABOUT IT TOO...

...HE WAS ALL, "HEY, LOOK WHAT YOUR NEW BOYFRIEND IS UP TO." UGH.

...

...BOYFRIEND.

GREAT.

MAYBE *HE'S* THE WEASEL!

HE'S GONNA TELL ME *EVERYTHING*!

LIV, WAIT...!

UH.

...

U-UM.

I-I...

GROWL

...REALLY? STOMACH?! *NOW?!*

...

...

GROWL

...

...

DO YOU WANNA EAT LUNCH?

HWOOOo.

...

WHISPER
GOSSIP

why's she sitting with him?

...

...!

H-HEY, QUIT IT!

IT WASN'T *HIM* IN THAT CHAT! SOMEONE *HACKED* HIM!

...!

GOSSIP ABOUT *THAT!*

...

...

...

U-UM...

I JUST WANNA SAY...

...I'M REALLY GLAD IT WASN'T YOU.

I...I WAS SO UPSET.

BUT THE FIRST THING I THOUGHT, WHEN I SAW IT, WAS ACTUALLY...

"NO WAY. NOT JORGE. THAT CAN'T BE HIM."

...

I SHOULD'VE TRUSTED MY GUT MORE, I GUESS.

. . .

D-DO YOU...

DO YOU REALLY KNOW WHO DID THAT TO YOU?

...

YEAH.

H-HOW COME YOU WON'T TELL WHO IT IS?

IS IT ONE OF JAMES'S GOONS?

THEY ARE *SO* NOT WORTH COVERING FOR.

UH...

*...I REALLY WANT TO TELL HER EVERYTHING.*

...

...

"*NO, IT WAS A FRIEND WHO HAS NO SPINE AND MAKES BAD LIFE DECISIONS.*"

...I SAW JAMES IN THE CAFETERIA. HE'S NOT EVEN *SORRY*, STRUTTING AROUND LIKE HE'S THE BEST.

...

AT LEAST NOW, NO ONE THINKS HE'S COOL ANYMORE.

...

...YOU'RE NOT EATING! IS YOUR SANDWICH OKAY?

DO YOU WANT SOME OF MY STUFF?

...

I'VE GOT SAMOSAS, CHICKEN SKEWERS, OHH, AND THIS IS...

RIGHT NOW, IT FEELS LIKE THE WHOLE WORLD IS AGAINST ME...

...BUT...

...AS LONG AS SHE'S ON MY SIDE...

...SOMEHOW, IT'S OKAY.

*BZZT*

ATTENTION, EVERYONE.

WOULD THE FOLLOWING STUDENTS PLEASE REPORT TO THE PRINCIPAL'S OFFICE IMMEDIATELY —

JAMES CORDEN, COLE HART, SAM REEVES, NATE BURNER...

...AND JORGE RUIZ.

....!

...WHAT?!

NO. NO, NO, NO.

TIC TOC TIC TOC

....!

WH-WHAT DID THEY SAY?

UH.

THEY'RE...

...STARTING AN INVESTIGATION. GONNA PULL UP THE CHAT LOGS AND READ THROUGH 'EM.

IF STUFF THEY FIND IS AS BAD AS IT LOOKS...

....!

...SUSPENSIONS FOR EVERYONE. WITH A MARK ON THE PERMANENT RECORD.

D-DID YOU TELL THEM IT WASN'T *YOU*?!

...NO.

YOU *HAVE* TO TELL THEM! IT WASN'T YOUR FAULT!

RRRING

....!

LUNCH IS OVER.

HUG

....!

T-TEXT ME, OKAY?

IF I CAN HELP...LET ME KNOW.

O-OKAY.

....

...!

...LIV.

H-HEY, UH, YOU OKAY?

...

I...

...I TALKED TO ZEKE.

HE...HE SAID...

...THAT HE GOT THE SCREENSHOTS FROM...FROM RON...

YOU KNOW, THE SMALL, SKINNY KID WHO HANGS OUT WITH JAMES?

THEY MAKE FUN OF HIM A LOT?

SO I WENT AND TALKED TO HIM TOO...

. . .

WAS IT REALLY GARRETT...?

Y-YES.

FLINCH

. . .

I-IT WAS AN ACCIDENT, THOUGH!

HE DIDN'T KNOW HE WAS LOGGED IN AS ME AT FIRST!

. . .

AND HE'S JUST... HE'S WATCHING YOU BURN?

FOR WHAT *HE* DID?

....!

HE DIDN'T MEAN TO!

*LIV!*

DON'T PROTECT HIM!

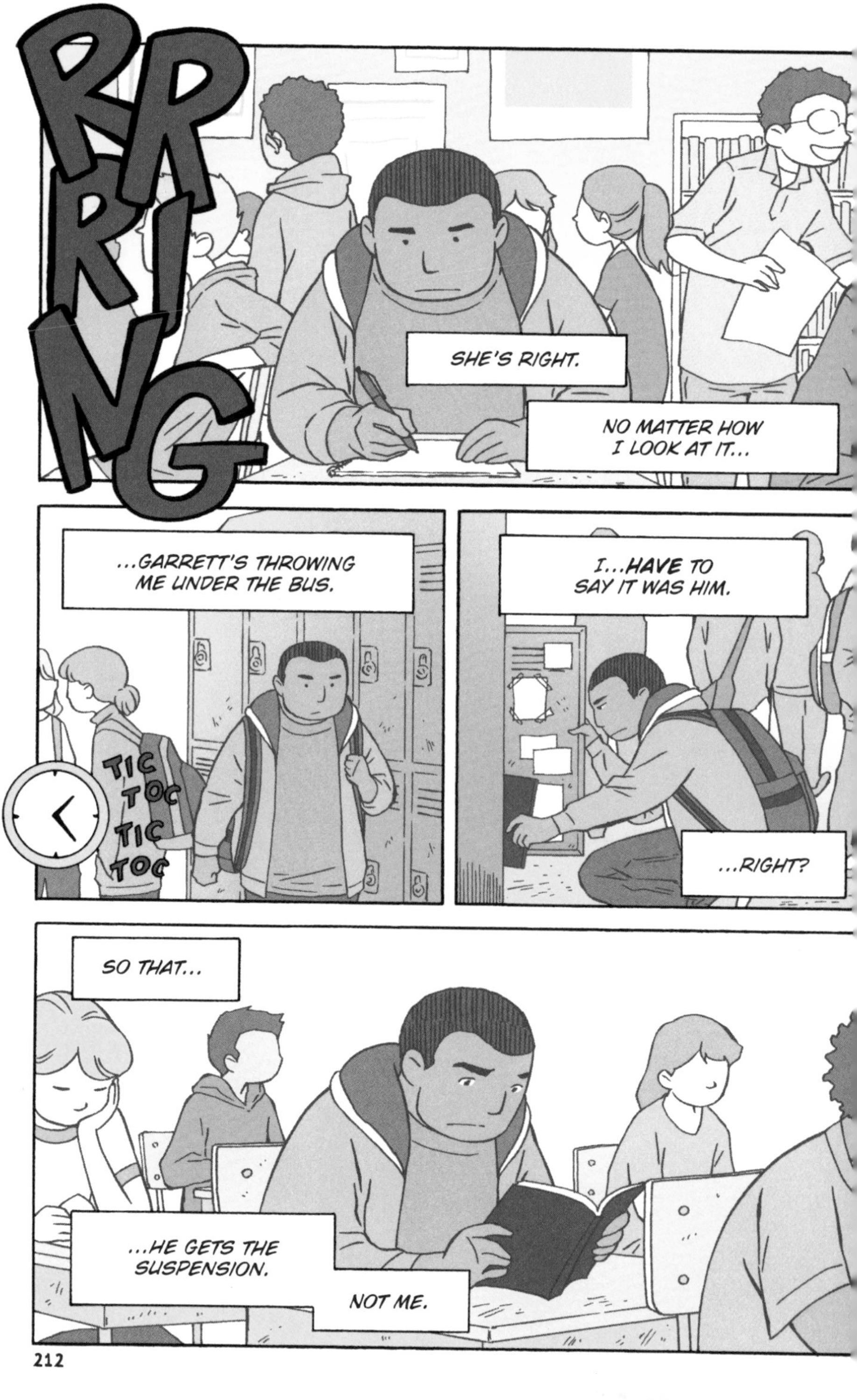
RRRRING
SHE'S RIGHT.
NO MATTER HOW I LOOK AT IT...
...GARRETT'S THROWING ME UNDER THE BUS.
TIC TOC TIC TOC
I...HAVE TO SAY IT WAS HIM.
...RIGHT?
SO THAT...
...HE GETS THE SUSPENSION.
NOT ME.

LOYAL JORGE... TELLING ON HIS FRIEND TO SAVE HIS OWN SKIN...

...

...

...

..."FRIEND."

CAN YOU COVER FOR ME?! LIV WILL KILL ME, HA-HA!

??

YOU DON'T NEED PRACTICE, HA-HA! I WANNA GO PLAY MADDEN!

YOU KEEP TAKING AND TAKING!! WHAT DO YOU GIVE BACK?!

TIC TOC TIC TOC

NNRGH.

* BZZT *

JORGE RUIZ TO THE PRINCIPAL'S OFFICE, PLEASE.

ALREADY?!

...

...

I THOUGHT THEY'D AT LEAST TAKE A DAY.

WHISPER

WHISPER

THIS IS NOT FAIR.

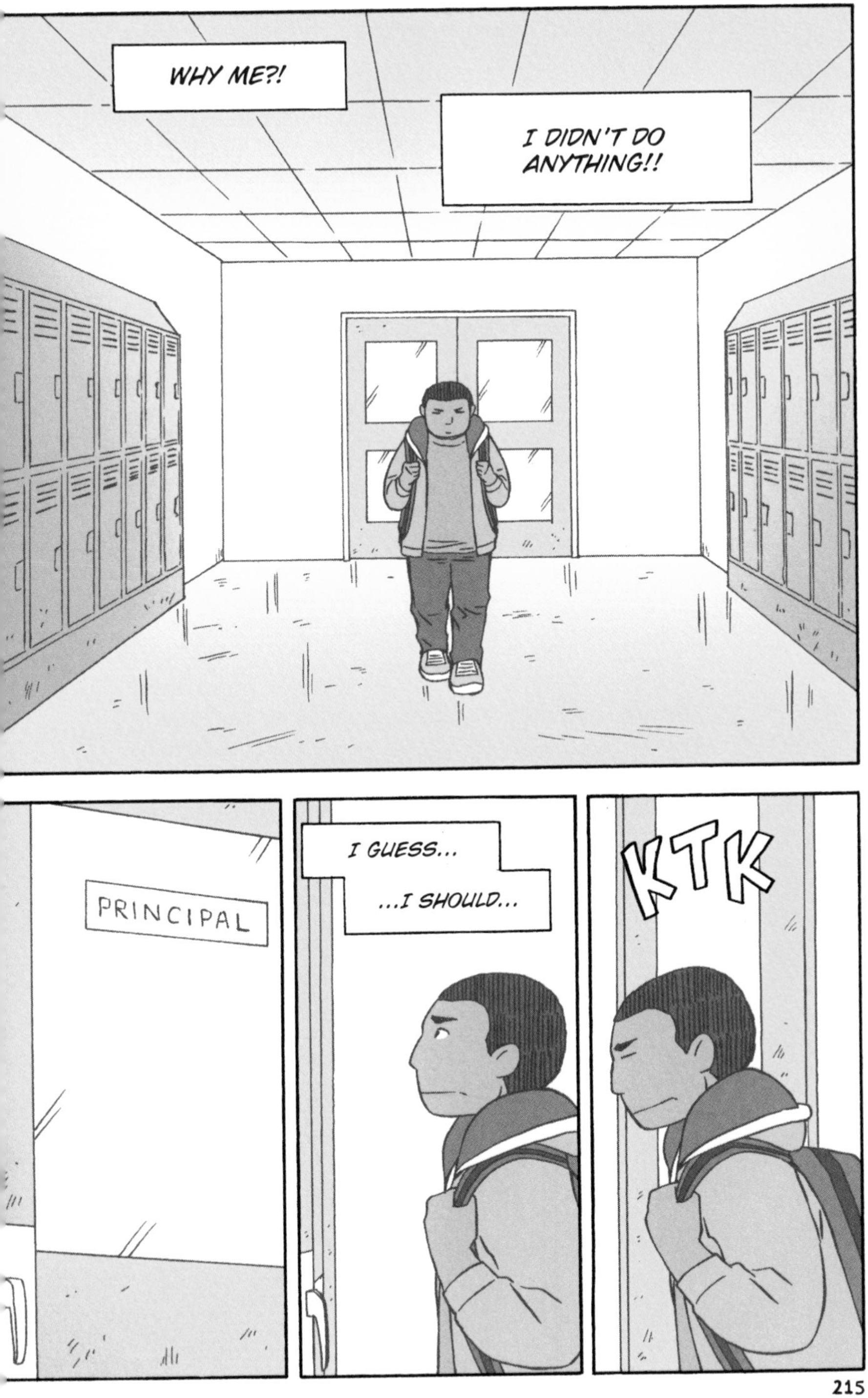
WHY ME?!
I DIDN'T DO ANYTHING!!
PRINCIPAL
I GUESS...
...I SHOULD...
KTK

....!

GARRETT?

AH, JORGE!

HAVE A SEAT. THEY'LL BE WITH YOU SHORTLY.

...WHAT IS HAPPENING?

WH-WHAT ARE YOU DOING HERE?

...

I TOLD THEM EVERYTHING.

ABOUT JAMES, ABOUT THE CHAT...

....!

...AND THAT YOU WEREN'T INVOLVED.

....!

...

I GUESS LIV GOT AHOLD OF YOU, HUH?

....!

LIV TRIED TO CALL ME?!

....!

CRAP.

MY PHONE'S BEEN OFF SINCE YESTERDAY.

I GOTTA FIND HER.

I SAID STUPID STUFF ABOUT HER IN THE CHAT.

GOTTA APOLOGIZE.

...HE...HE DID THIS ON HIS OWN. LIV DIDN'T MAKE HIM.

...

YOU WERE RIGHT ABOUT JAMES.

I SHOULD'VE LISTENED TO YOU.

I-I KNOW YOU PROBABLY HATE ME NOW.

BUT I JUST...

...

I'M SORRY.

I WAS A CRAPPY FRIEND.

...

JORGE?

GO ON IN, DEAR. THEY'RE READY FOR YOU.

....!

. . .

WHAT...

WHAT JUST EVEN HAPPENED?

# CHAPTER 11

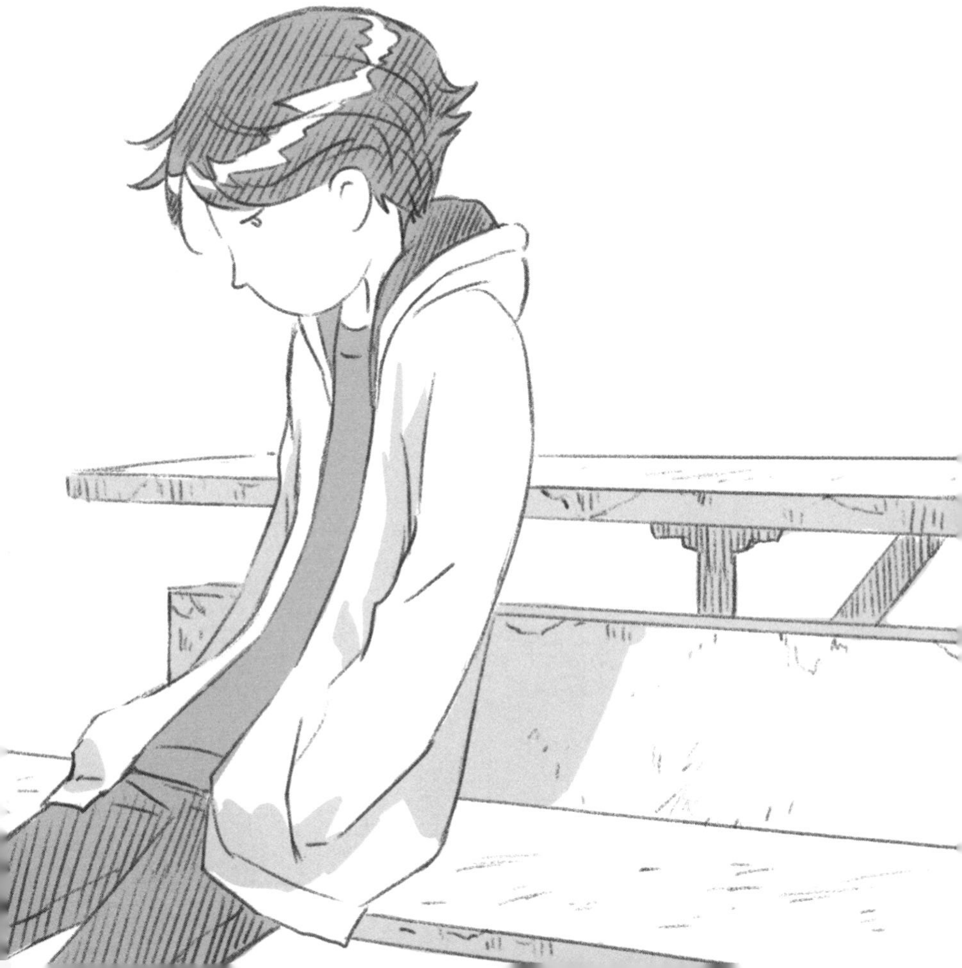

WHAT HAPPENED WAS GARRETT *DID* TELL EVERYTHING.

BERRYBROOK MIDDLE

TWO WEEKS LATER.

I GOT AN APOLOGY FROM THE PRINCIPAL.

AND JAMES GOT SUSPENDED SO HARD...

...ALONG WITH HIS CIRCUS MONKEYS.

MRS. RASHAD KICKED THEM OFF THE FOOTBALL TEAM TOO.

FWEET!

PICK UP THOSE KNEES!

(SHE WAS *LIVID* WHEN SHE FOUND OUT.)

SCHOOL'S, UH...

...KINDA BACK TO NORMAL, I GUESS?

SOME PEOPLE LOOK AT ME WEIRD.

BUT NO ONE HATES ME ANYMORE.

(I THINK.)

JORGE!!

CAN I BORROW THE PROJECT NOTES AGAIN?

...SURE.

YESSS! THANKS.

...UNTIL THE NEXT GOSSIP BLOWUP, I GUESS.

...

JORGE!!

SLAP

LUNCH WITH THE DRAMA PEEPS AGAIN!

COME ON, MOVE YOUR BUTT!

MAKE ME, BOSSY.

ha ha

LIKE I EVEN *HAVE* TO!

JAZMINE'S GONN[A] BE THERE!

...

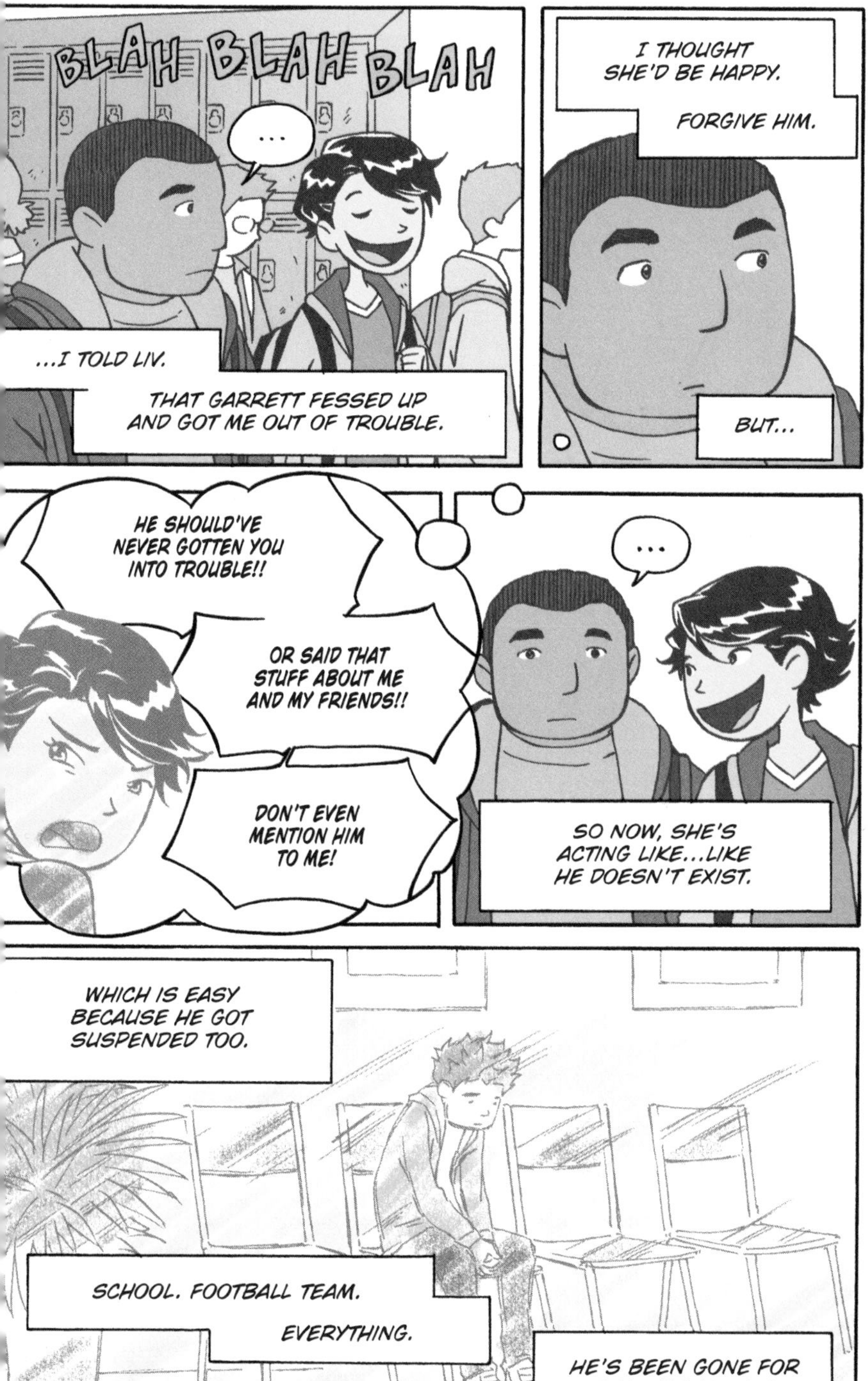
BLAH BLAH BLAH
...
...I TOLD LIV.
THAT GARRETT FESSED UP AND GOT ME OUT OF TROUBLE.
I THOUGHT SHE'D BE HAPPY.
FORGIVE HIM.
BUT...
HE SHOULD'VE NEVER GOTTEN YOU INTO TROUBLE!!
OR SAID THAT STUFF ABOUT ME AND MY FRIENDS!!
DON'T EVEN MENTION HIM TO ME!
...
SO NOW, SHE'S ACTING LIKE...LIKE HE DOESN'T EXIST.
WHICH IS EASY BECAUSE HE GOT SUSPENDED TOO.
SCHOOL. FOOTBALL TEAM.
EVERYTHING.
HE'S BEEN GONE FOR TWO WEEKS NOW.

SORRY FOR BEING A CRAPPY FRIEND.

...

...I KNOW WHAT HE DID **SUCKED**...

...BUT...

...SOMEHOW, I CAN'T HATE HIM.

LIV! JORGE! THERE YOU ARE!

I SAVED YOU GUYS SPOTS!

UGH, **FINALLY!**

NIIIIC...

ha ha

JORGE, TELL HER YOU DON'T WANT HER STUPID SPRING ROLLS!

WHA...?

haha

NIC WANTS MY SPRING ROLLS, BUT I WAS SAVING THEM FOR YOU.

IT'S NOT FAIR!!

YOU USED TO ALWAYS GIVE **ME** YOUR FOOD!

I HATE YOUR BOYFRIEND, JAZMINE!

UH.

I HAVE CHEESECAKE, IF YOU WANT IT.

...

...I LOVE YOUR BOYFRIEND, JAZMINE.

...NIC IS EASILY TAMED WITH FOOD, HUH?

...

..."BOYFRIEND."

HA HA HA

WE'VE BEEN HANGING OUT A LOT MORE.

WAVE

SHE COMES TO MY PRACTICE SOMETIMES...

...AND I HELP HER PRACTICE THE LINES FOR THEIR PLAY.

C-COULD YOU SPARE A CENT, KIND MISS?

*COUGH COUGH*

YOU'D NEVER KNOW IT...

WHY, ELIZA, DON'T YOU—

...BECAUSE SHE'S SO SHY WITH PEOPLE...

W
IST
RL
GC

...BUT SHE'S **AMAZING**.

OH!

BLESS YOU, MISS!

LIKE, SHE'S SO GOOD, SHE SHOULD BE IN MOVIES.

YOU SHOULD BE IN **MOVIES**.

TH-THANKS!

ha ha

...FIRST, I HAVE TO NOT BOMB ON THE SCHOOL STAGE...I GET SO NERVOUS...

...SHE'S GONNA KICK ALL THE AVAILABLE BUTT IN THAT PLAY.

LIFE FEELS LIKE
A PERFECT MOVIE
RIGHT NOW...

BECAUSE ZEKE IS
STILL AROUND, BEING
A SACK OF WEASELS.

...BUT I KNOW
IT'S NOT.

(AND RUNNING THE
YEARBOOK CLUB.)

...AND BECAUSE LIV IS SAD.

SHE PUTS UP A
GOOD FRONT...

HEY!

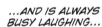
...AND IS ALWAYS
BUSY LAUGHING...

...BUT IT'S
NOT...

...REAL.

SHE WANTED TO HANG OUT TODAY, JUST THE TWO OF US.

IT'S BEEN A WHILE... I WAS STARTING TO WORRY.

I MEAN...

...I ALREADY LOST ONE BEST FRIEND.

WEIRD SHE WANTED TO MEET HERE.

SHE'S BEEN AVOIDING THIS PLACE EVER SINCE...

...GARRETT—

....!

....!

GARRETT?!

H-HEY, MAN!

ARE...ARE YOU BACK?

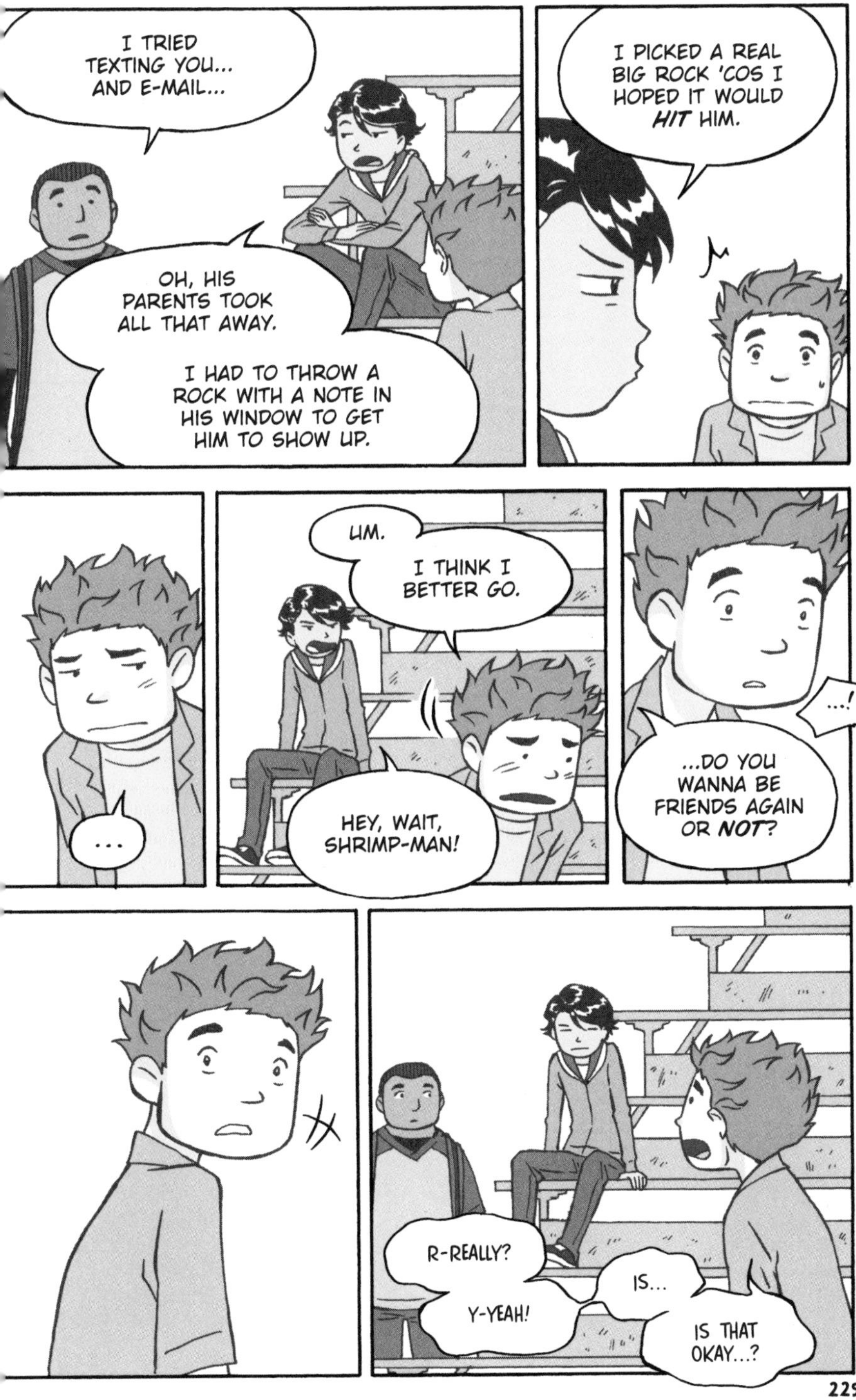
I TRIED TEXTING YOU... AND E-MAIL...
OH, HIS PARENTS TOOK ALL THAT AWAY.
I HAD TO THROW A ROCK WITH A NOTE IN HIS WINDOW TO GET HIM TO SHOW UP.
I PICKED A REAL BIG ROCK 'COS I HOPED IT WOULD HIT HIM.
...
UM.
I THINK I BETTER GO.
HEY, WAIT, SHRIMP-MAN!
...DO YOU WANNA BE FRIENDS AGAIN OR NOT?
...!
R-REALLY?
Y-YEAH!
IS...
IS THAT OKAY...?

WELL, FIRST OF ALL— I'M ONLY DOING THIS FOR JORGE...

....

...WHO IS A PRECIOUS, PURE CINNAMON ROLL, APPARENTLY, AND CAN'T HOLD A GRUDGE AGAINST YOU.

PRETTY SURE HE'S TAKING YOU BACK AS IS.

BUT ME?

I GOT *CONDITIONS.*

LIKE...

...YOU *HAVE* TO APOLOGIZE TO JAZMINE AND BROOKE AND *ME* FOR ALL THE STUPID STUFF YOU SAID.

YES!! I'M SO SORRY! I DIDN'T MEAN ANY—

*AND* YOU HAVE TO DO YOUR OWN HOMEWORK!

AND ALSO...

...

....!

AND ANOTHER THING...

*I THOUGHT LIV WAS DONE WITH HIM.*

IS... IS THIS REALLY HAPPENING?

ARE THEY MAKING UP...?

YEAH.

OKAY.

YEP.

GARRETT WAS BACK IN SCHOOL TWO DAYS LATER.

ERRYBROOK MIDDLE SCHOOL

HE DIDN'T LIE— HIS HOMEWORK WAS DONE...

...AND HE DID GO AROUND AND APOLOGIZE TO THE GIRLS.

HMPF

WHATEVER.

NOT OF ALL THEM WERE IMPRESSED, BUT...

...LIV WAS.

...OKAY, GOOD ENOUGH!

WELCOME BACK, SHRIMP-MAN!

THAT'S WHAT MATTERED, REALLY.

COME ON, I GOT SO MUCH TO SHOW YOU!!

I KNOW SHE SAID SHE WAS JUST DOING IT FOR ME...

HA HA HA

OMG!

...BUT I THINK SHE MISSED THIS IDIOT TOO.

...EVEN THOUGH THE TWO OF THEM ARE BASICALLY A NEVER-ENDING WRESTLING MATCH.

...

TAKE JIU-JITSU WITH ME.

ugh, no.

DO IT.

make me.

REMEMBER HOW I SAID LIFE IS MORE COMPLICATED THAN SPORTS?

IT'LL THROW A LOT OF CURVEBALLS AT YOU.

YOU WIN SOME GAMES AND LOSE OTHERS...

...BUT IN THE END, IT'S WHO'S ON YOUR TEAM THAT REALLY MATTERS.

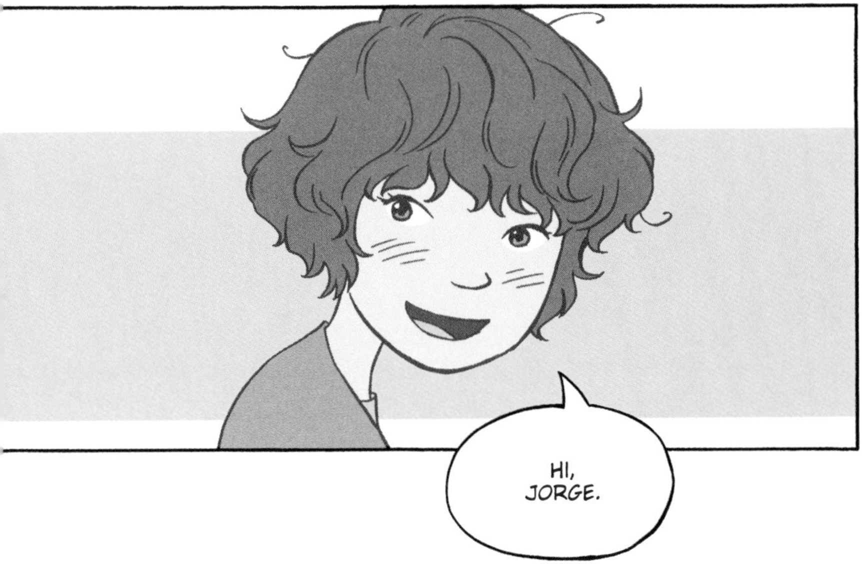
HI, JORGE.

THE END

... Hello, there! WE MEET AGAIN! 😊

(... or we meet for the first
time, in which case HI,
I have made other books
that you can read. 😊)

**crush** was a book I've been SO excited to writ
I don't know about you, but I had such huge crush
on people in middle school. All of them secret, beca
unlike Jorge, I was too shy to ask my crush out. So I
just admired them from afar... Until I found out tha
my crush was actually kind of a mean and jerky person. ☹
Which is when I stopped crushing on them and started
silently judging them from afar. 😒 Needless to say,
my love life in middle school did not work out as well
as Jorge's... OH WELL.

It takes a lot of work to
make a graphic novel, and I try to
always start with rough
character designs so that I
always have some reference to
look to, when I am drawing the
actual comic pages.
Sometimes characters change
a lot once I start drawing them
in the comic! And sometimes they
stay the same. Either way, it's
REALLY helpful to go through
this design process before
diving into the sequential art.

Jorge Ruiz

Olivia Hoffman    Garrett Brock    Jazmine Duong

BACKPACKS

Jorge    Olivia

.. never thought I'd need a cheat sheet for backpacks, and yet here it is. So Many Backpacks! I couldn't remember who had which design, so having this model sheet really helped during the page-drawing stage.

Jazmine    Garrett    Zeke    James

# THE EVOLUTION OF A PANEL:

A book panel ALWAYS starts as a tiny rough sketch first. Once my editor and I are sure that the panel works, I draw the pencils (a larger, tighter version of the panel), which I then print out in non-photo blue for inking!

(During the inking stage, I sometimes change and add things — like Jorge's smile and Mr. Raccoon, here.)

Once the panel is inked, it is colored digitally, to make it ready for print. Ta-dah! Now I just have to do this 1,200 more times and I will have a book!

(... comics are a lot of work...)

## THE EVOLUTION OF A COVER:

Cover is a really important part of the book because it's the first thing people see. I usually try out several sketches...

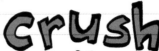

Before I land on the winner...

That will become the cover!

# ☆ THANK YOU! ☆

As I mentioned, making graphic novels is a lot of work, but the production of this one was especially difficult becau in the middle of it all, I became a mom to this little guy.

As I crawl over the finish line, I feel immense gratitude to the people that helped me get here.

JuYoun

Patrick

Ruth

Melissa

NaRae

Bon

YEN PRESS PRODUCTION CREW

THANK YOOOOU

With lots of tired hugs,

Svet~

Aug. 26 2018